Mittelschmerz

Mittelschmerz

A Novel

Caryn Bark

To Julie

Caryn Bark

WRP
West Ridge Press
Chicago

Published by West Ridge Press
West Ridge Press
Chicago, Illinois, USA

www.westridgepress.com

First Printing, July 2006

Library of Congress 2006926968

ISBN 0-9786051-0-1

Printed in the United States of a America

10 9 8 7 6 5 4 3 2 1

This is dedicated to my parents, Sid and Shirley Bark, who always encourage me and always have faith in me.

Many thanks to my first readers, Marla Dembitz and B. James (who blackmailed me into writing daily). Special thanks to my girls-of-summer. They are the best. Thanks to Betty Mohr for her enthusiastic encouragement. Thank you to my three children, who are an endless source of material, and to my loving husband Fred, who never ceases to amaze me. I am also grateful to the folks at West Ridge Press, especially my talented editor Efraim Ben David. I feel truly blessed to be surrounded by so many supportive friends and family members.

CHAPTER ONE

The invitation arrived exactly six weeks in advance, conforming to the accepted standard for proper length of time before the event. It was just like Lillian to do everything by the rules. She always gave the correct notice prior to any party she threw, just as she always started studying in advance during our years at the University of Illinois.

I, on the other hand, always pulled last minute all-nighters. Currently, I owe several thank-you notes that are way overdue to say nothing of my late fees for the Chicago Public Library and Blockbuster Video Stores.

Lillian had a handle on proper etiquette but was still a fun girl in our sorority days and could party with the best of them. She had a short failed marriage to a depressed accountant that produced a darling little girl, whom I estimated to be about twenty by now. I had heard Lillian was dating Barry Ladman, whom I knew peripherally as a second or third cousin to my soon-to-be ex-husband Marv. The eggshell embossed invitation, which I noticed was in perfect taste for a second marriage (on both sides), confirmed that they had indeed been involved and were now taking this one step further. I put the invitation and response card in my writing desk drawer. I very much wanted to attend this event but was concerned whether Marv would be there. I made a mental note to call Lillian in a few weeks to find out.

I got a call from Mitzi, another sorority sister, who lives in Minneapolis. We're all part of a group from the AEPhi sorority house at the University of Illinois that tries to get together every summer and go to Lake Geneva for a weekend. Lillian has attended on and off, but Mitzi and I have been to every one of those weekends.

"You're going aren't you? Because I'm definitely coming in town for this. Have you ever met this Barry?" she inquired.

"Don't you remember, he's Marv's cousin? Not a first cousin but they were close growing up," I told her.

"Will he be there?" Mitzi asked.

"I have no idea."

"Well, you have to haul ass and find out. 'Cause if he's there, and especially if he's there with a date, you'd better find yourself a date. You're not staying home when we're all getting together for this."

"Is Allen coming in with you?" I asked.

"No, he can't. Tax season," Mitzi said.

"So, you'll be my date."

"Come on. If I had a husband who left me, I'd show up dressed to the nines with some hunky guy."

"I don't have to impress Marv," I said.

"I know, but I mean, do this for yourself. Just think about it. And if you can't find anyone we'll go together and have a great time. But give it some thought."

"I'd love a date, but I've told you, I already know every available Jewish man over forty-five in the greater Chicagoland Metropolitan area," I admitted.

I wasn't looking to impress Marv, and I didn't even know yet if he would be going to the wedding, but for some reason, I started going to as many Yoga classes as I could fit into my schedule. I had originally started attending Yoga classes about six months after Marv and I broke up. The first six months I ate as if every meal was the midnight buffet on the QE II. I didn't exercise. I drove the kids to their activities while munching in the car. I wrote my columns but mostly from home and hardly ever went into the office.

Suddenly, I realized I had packed on twenty-five pounds. This was not helpful. To be dumped was none of my doing, but to become dumpy was in the realm of my own control. I would have to concentrate on looking my best. I started slowly with Yoga and watched what I ate. Before I knew it, I had not only taken off the twenty-five pounds but also another five. Even my kids took notice.

"Mom's looking hot," chided Agatha, my fourteen-year-old, one morning. I had gotten up extra early that day and didn't like the way my kinky brown hair looked. I took Agatha's sewing scissors and started hacking off my hair. I cut it super short. It looked really youthful and hip. It was too short to curl, but it waved in all different directions.

I threw on big, silver hoop earrings and some shiny lip gloss. Delilah, my five-year-old, agreed that I looked hot and even Drake, my seventeen-year-old son, added, "Well, not hot. No offense Mom, that would be gross. But you look pretty okay." That was the most he'd spoken to me since he had turned fifteen.

I hadn't felt that good in a long time. Now, Mitzi was encouraging me to get a date for Lillian's wedding, and I had to admit it wasn't such a bad idea, even if Marv wasn't going to attend. However, I would know the answer to that riddle soon enough because, the following week, I received a phone call from Lillian for the distinct purpose of relaying that information.

"Linda, I hope you're coming to my wedding. Everyone's coming: Mitzi, Caro, Jen, Doree—the whole group—but I wanted you to know in advance that Marv sent in his response card. He's going to be there."

"I appreciate you letting me know, and believe me, I will be there. It doesn't bother me at all," I told Lillian.

"I'm glad to hear that. I guess you two have a pretty good relationship because of the kids," she said.

"We're definitely civil," I told her.

"That's best. But I also wanted to let you know he's bringing a date," she informed me.

"I was wondering about that," I admitted.

"He told Barry he's bringing someone. He didn't say it's serious or anything, but I just thought you should know he won't be alone. You should bring someone," Lillian suggested.

Those were the same exact words Katherine, my editor, used when we discussed this wedding in her office the next day. Katherine has been in the newspaper business forever and knows everyone there is to know. So, I wasn't too surprised when she suggested helping.

"I could set you up. In fact, I know a big fan of yours. He'd love to escort you," Katherine said.

"I know I should go with someone, but it would be so awkward."

"Not at all. The person I have in mind will put you right at ease," she said.

"So, who is this person?" I asked.

"Patrick."

"As in Patrick Rainey the Fourth?" I asked.

"I've told you what a great guy he is."

She was referring to her stepson. Katherine had discussed him with me many times. They have a very close relationship. She's still married to Patrick Rainey the Third but he's retired and spends most of his time in their Palm Springs home. Patrick the Fourth lives in Chicago and is the CEO of a mid-sized consulting firm. I've spotted his name in the Tribune's *About Town* column numerous times.

"He wouldn't want to go to a total stranger's wedding with me, another total stranger," I said.

"On the contrary, he loves your columns. We discuss the paper all the time. He thinks you have a biting sense of humor, and he likes older women—never dates women his own age. Just think about it."

I promised Katherine I would mull it over. I kept thinking about it, so much so, that I began discussing it with all the acquaintances in my life. Mrs. Park, my Korean dry cleaner, thought I should stay home and not make waves, but her daughter Kim disagreed. She felt her mom is too old fashioned, too old world.

"Get with it Mom. She should go and bring some hot guy. Know any hot guy?" Kim asked me.

"Not really," I answered as I lugged my newly cleaned sweaters and blazers over my shoulder out of her shop.

LaShanda, my favorite check-out clerk at the Jewel Food Store, definitely thought I should go and with a date.

"Girl, you are looking hot, and you should haul your booty to that wedding, and if you want to show up with some big, buffed, caramel-skinned brother, I can arrange that too," she said. I politely passed on her offer.

"Maybe he's not bringing a date, and the two of you can go together," was Susan's suggestion. Susan is my longtime friend from college and my attorney. I felt she was stalling on my divorce.

"He's bringing someone. And where is that paperwork we're waiting for?"

"I told you. His attorney is out of town," Susan said.

"Again? Doesn't he have any associates?" I asked.

"One-man office. Small-time stuff. These cinnamon buns are great. Try some." Sue shoved a forkful towards me.

We were lunching at Ann Sather's on Clark Street. Sue was on her breakfast diet. She could eat anything she wanted as long as it was in the breakfast category.

"Listen to that family order," she said. I overheard them ordering pancakes, milk, bacon, sausage, more orders of milk, and ham.

"They're so *goyish*," she remarked.

I always get a kick out of Sue, who is Catholic, but talks like she's Jewish. She grew up in a Catholic neighborhood, then came to the University of Illinois, and lived in Bromley Hall, the private dorm where all the northside Jewish kids lived. She hung out with Jewish girls, dated Jewish boys, and became the Sweetheart of ZBT.

Sue was still eavesdropping on the family's order and making faces as their requests of pancakes and pork products appeared to have no end.

"I've seen you eat bacon," I remarked.

"Yes but never with milk," was her reply. "Do you ever feel low about losing your looks?" she asked me.

"Am I losing my looks?" I was concerned by her remark.

"No, actually you look terrific. But I mean in general— our getting older. We still look great, but things are starting to go in all different directions. Do you ever get sad thinking about it?" she asked.

"Sometimes. I look at our old photos from Bromley Hall. God we were adorable. Those full faces and slim hips."

"Tight chins and good arms," Sue added to my list.

"Exactly. But then I think how grateful I am for everything, even with Marv leaving," I said.

"I know what you mean. Remember that New Year's Eve at my apartment on East Scott Street?" she asked.

"We were thirty and worried that we couldn't find anyone to marry, and we'd miss out on having kids," I remembered.

"Things'll work out," she murmured.

"What'll work out? My divorce?"

"Yeah, sure, everything. You know, as soon as Marv's attorney gets back."

"I still have this feeling you're stalling," I said.

"No, but Linda, who knows what'll happen between now and then?" she asked while filling her mouth with yet another gooey cinnamon bun.

Chapter Two

My *friend Laurie started meeting me at Yoga class. We first met when our boys were in preschool together at the Bernard Horwich Jewish Community Center. "You're so skinny," Laurie commented as we were putting our mats away.*

"You only think that 'cause you're looking at my legs. You're not looking at my stomach or breasts." She always does this because Laurie's the type of Jewish woman who is thin on top—long swanlike neck, small breasts, long flat tummy and waist, but from there, things take a turn—wide hips, bulky thighs, thick legs. I am the opposite—buxom with long thin legs. Women like Laurie only see my thin legs, but I only see their flat tummies.

"It's better than being big on the bottom," Laurie suggested.

"I don't think so. You can dress to hide your flaws," I said.

"I'm tired of always wearing long skirts and boots."

"They're very flattering," I told her.

"You know what Matthew used to call my legs? Cankles," she said.

"Cankles?" I asked.

"Yeah, calf-ankles," she explained.

Matthew is her ex-husband. And I knew what she meant. She has those really thick shapeless legs that go straight into her shoes. That's why she always wears boots.

"Sometimes he'd call me No-Knees 'cause my legs go so straight," Laurie said.

"The weird thing is Matthew's new wife has the same legs," Laurie told me.

"You get along with her, right?" I asked.

"She's great. Actually, I have the best of both worlds. I have my kids, my house, child support, and every weekend, Matthew takes the boys, and I can go out. It beats marriage."

From Laurie's point of view, divorce looked great—all the benefits of marriage, plus you can date. As for myself, it was true, I was still in our marital house even though Marv had purchased it when he was single. My finances hadn't changed. I continued to have control of our joint bank account because I was always the one in charge of writing the checks. And, like Laurie's husband Mathew, Marv took the kids on the weekends. The only difference between Laurie and me was that I wasn't making use of my weekends to go out. I was usually working on my column on the weekends.

"So, who are you taking to that wedding? You are going, right?" Laurie inquired.

Our Yoga class had ended, and we were in the club steam room, our bodies *shvitzing* and our hair frizzing.

"My editor wants me to take her stepson," I told her.

"Really, what's he like?" she asked.

"I don't know," I admitted. "I've never met him. He's young, good-looking—I've seen his picture—successful. His name is Patrick Rainey the Fourth."

"Wow. I've never been out with a Fourth. I've never even met a Fourth, or a Third, or a Second for that matter. Sounds like a total WASP. He's perfect to show up with at the wedding," she said.

I had to admit. He was starting to sound like a great revenge date. We stepped out of the steam room and headed to the showers passing the mirrors. I stopped.

"Look at my hair," I said. It had turned into a short afro but Laurie, who also has kinky hair, although long, had now sprouted a huge afro.

"Yours? Look at me. I'm like the Jewish Angela Davis. I hope I still have some Frizz-Control in my bag. Aren't I blessed — cankles and an Is-fro," Laurie complained.

She was referring to Jewish Afros. We had several terms for them–Is-fro (as in Israel), Heb-fro (Hebrew), and Jew-fro (self explanatory).

"Don't worry I've got some Murray's AfroGel with me," I said.

"Thank goodness. I couldn't find it at the Jewel last time."

"I know they've moved the aisles around, and I can't find anything," I told her.

"I hate when they do that."

CHAPTER THREE

I was at, what I generously refer to as, my office – a cubicle in the Northside News office on Lincoln Avenue. I had gotten quite a bit of e-mail regarding a recent **Shades of Grey** column dealing with recreation time. My point was that many people are working extra hours so that they can hire more help to do the cleaning, gardening, auto maintenance, etc. Then they need to join a club so that they can workout to get in shape when all they had to do was those chores, and they could work less hours. Plus, they have to pay for their health club fees, and they waste time traveling to and from the club.

I was trying to decide which letters to print in a follow up column when I spotted it among the e-mails I had been reading on my desktop.

Dear Ms. Grey,
Your column about recreation time really hit home. I've been rushing around the city in cabs hoping to get my workday finished in time to go to the gym

and walk the track. After reading your column, I've decided to walk to and from the office, to all my meetings, and appointments and not worry about getting to the track. It turns out I'm walking about five miles each day. I've encouraged my employees to do the same. They've cut their taxi expenses and are feeling great. Most important, it gives us all time to notice our surroundings and enjoy this great city. I also found an unusual cafe you might want to write about — Cafe Kotel.

Patrick Rainey

I thought it was odd that Katherine's husband would send me an e-mail, so I printed it out and walked into her office to get her take on it. Katherine was doing the New York Times crossword puzzle. Without even looking up to see who had entered her office she asked, "What's an eight letter word for big deal?"

"I don't know, oh, Megillah."

"Linda, you're brilliant." She took off her rhinestone rimmed reading glasses and looked up at me. "What's up?"

I handed her the printed e-mail. Katherine read it and said, "He's told me about that place. You should go see it."

"Isn't it odd. Your husband e-mailing me?" I asked.

"Good Lord Linda. That's not from Paddie. It's from Patrick."

"Oh," I said.

"All that talk about office and employees. You know Paddie's retired. He spends his time golfing and digging into those dusty old mariner's maps."

"I wasn't thinking about the content of the letter. When I saw the name I just thought of Patrick the Third. Why didn't he sign it the Fourth?"

"Patrick feels it's pretentious to put a number after his name. I told you he's a fan. He wants to show you that cafe," she said.

"He wants me to see the place, and he's willing to go to the wedding with me?" I said.

"I haven't mentioned that yet. He just wants to take you there," Katherine told me.

"But that's an odd coincidence. You want me to take him on my revenge date, but you haven't mentioned it to Patrick, and he just happens to write to me." I had summed it up.

"Not really such a coincidence. I told you he's a fan of yours. He knows you're separated, so why shouldn't he make contact?" she asked.

I wasn't buying it. I felt Katherine put him up to it, but I played along.

"So, what am I supposed to do now? E-mail him back?"

"You can, but knowing Patrick, he'll most likely call you. Maybe even today," she said.

I stayed at the office all day—much longer than I normally do. I figured I could get work done since Delilah had her Brownie meeting after school, and I didn't have to pick her up until five-thirty. But I hardly got any work accomplished. I was secretly hoping to get that call from Patrick Rainey the Fourth, not out of any interest in him personally, but if I could line him up as a date for Lillian's wedding, I'd have all that pressure lifted, my friends would stop hounding me, and I could drop my wool slacks at the cleaners without the fear of Kim offering to introduce me to some sexy Tae Kwan Do master.

The next day the kids went off to school as usual, Agatha yelling, "Love you Mom," as she ran out the door with wet hair, Delilah gave me a big hug as her carpool pulled up, and Drake ran out the door without a word, chugging a can of highly caffeinated Red Bull, no hug, kiss, or even a goodbye for his mom.

"I love you, too," I yelled after him.

I was straightening out the house which, by the time the kids leave, always looks like a trailer park somewhere in southern Illinois after a tornado has been through town. Delilah's Barbie and Ken dolls were all over the house. They have dozens of outfits, but for some reason, they're usually naked, cluttered in piles. And I noticed they were in some intriguing positions, which I recognized as the handiwork of Agatha. Drake left a plate of half eaten waffles and an empty can of Red Bull by his bed. In Agatha's room, I could see that she couldn't decide which skirt to wear because they had all been taken out of her drawers and were on the floor around her bed.

I had some errands to run before heading into the office, and I mentally made a note to add stopping by Dipti's for an eyebrow threading. I had been putting this off, but now worried that I might run into Patrick Rainey the Fourth and didn't want to be mistaken for Groucho Marx the Second (although I doubted if Mr. the Fourth was even old enough to know who Groucho Marx was).

"You haven't been here in two months. I told you every three weeks. I think you touched these yourself." Dipti was talking to me with the thread hanging from between her teeth.

I was hoping she wouldn't notice that I had waxed my brows myself some weeks earlier and hadn't completed the job, so that now they were growing in in an unusual pattern.

"Linda, you are not allowed to touch these. Only Dipti!" She reprimanded me in her Indian-accented English while pulling my unwanted eyebrow hairs out by stretching thread around them. One end of the two threads was between her teeth as she yanked the other end. It was quick and not quite painless.

She shoved a mirror in my face—two perfectly arched eyebrows—it was like an instant mini face-lift. I placed a ten dollar bill in the cardboard cigar box on the vanity. "Next," she yelled and a hairy young Pakistani man jumped into the barber's chair that I had previously been occupying.

Dipti has two barber chairs and a waiting line in her storefront threading business. Everyone takes a number and she spends about forty-five seconds with each client. I figured out since Dipti makes ten dollars every forty-five seconds and always has a line of hirsute folks waiting, she is possibly the richest woman in Chicago outside of Oprah Winfrey.

I stopped at the dry cleaners to drop off my wool pants. Kim waited on me. "Your face looks alert. You have something done?" she asked.

"I was just at Dipti's," I explained.

"Good brows. How about I introduce you to someone?"

Some good-looking Tai Kwan Do Master, I thought.

"My Uncle Dojo. He handsome. And he black belt in Hap Ki Do."

"No thanks. I think I'm going to meet my editor's stepson. She wants me to take him to the wedding."

"Sounds good. What's he like?" Kim asked.

"I don't know. One of those Something, Something the Fourths."

"A WASP. Perfect."

CHAPTER FOUR

I got into my office/cubby and began working on a story about how kids today are over-scheduled. As I sat writing it, I realized my kids aren't over-scheduled, but that I was being over-scheduled. I was deep in thought when the phone rang. I answered it and was surprised to discover it was Mr. The Fourth. I had forgotten about him as I had been in the Zone with my writing.

"Ms. Grey? This is Patrick Rainey."

"The Fourth?" I asked.

"I don't really like to use numbers or titles."

"I mean. This isn't the Third."

"No. Absolutely not the Third. I can't even read a map. I hope I'm not bothering you. I know how writers can get into a writing mode, and I'd hate to interrupt that."

"Not at all. I was just making a grocery list." I had made that up off the top of my head. I never use grocery lists which is why, when I leave the Jewel, I always discover that I've bought everything except what I had originally come for.

"Good. I was hoping you could meet me for lunch at the Cafe Kotel. It's really unusual."

"You think it would make a good story?" I asked.

"I do, but I would really like to meet you and have lunch."

"And it's a nice day for a walk," I said. I had noticed all of the previous weeks snow had melted.

"It's a one mile walk from my office, four blocks from yours."

"I thought you can't read maps," I said.

"True, but I'm not directionally challenged, and I know how you advocate walking in the city," he said.

Directionally challenged was a term I recognized from one of my past articles and *walking in the city* was a reference to my story about recreational time. So, Patrick really was a fan. That felt good.

The Cafe Kotel was located on a narrow side street off of Lincoln Avenue. It was a small storefront cozily tucked between an occult bookstore and a violin repair shop. The cafe was fashioned after Jerusalem's Kotel — Western Wall. There were only about ten tables, mostly four tops with wooden chairs, and a few two tops with cozy cushy chairs. The interior walls were exposed brick. There were spaces between some bricks with little pieces of paper sticking out. Most of the tables were filled with all kinds of people: students, business men and women, mothers and daughters, a group of elderly women. The waiters looked to be young art student types. They were serving Middle Eastern fare to the customers.

Sitting alone at a four top in the back near the kitchen holding a magnificent pink Gerber daisy was an elegant young man whom I figured to be Patrick. I recognized him from his photos in the *About Town* column. I walked over to his table, and he stood up. He was taller than I had expected, broad-shouldered, and trim. He had curly blondish-brown hair and green eyes. He smiled flashing large white teeth and handed me the flower. I took it and sat down.

"Thank you. It's beautiful. I love Gerber daisies."

"To harken the coming of spring. Isn't that what the

poets say?" he asked.

"Something to that effect," I answered. Just then a dark, handsome, middle-aged man came over to our table. He was accompanied by a young waiter who placed small glasses in front of us and began to pour mint tea very dramatically from a samovar.

"Welcome," he greeted us. "Patrick, so glad to see you." He had a slight accent that sounded Israeli. Patrick introduced me to Habib, the owner, who, it turns out, is an Israeli Bedouin.

I noticed that many of the patrons were writing notes on scraps of paper and sticking them in the cracks of the wall. Habib started to explain. "Just like the Kotel in Jerusalem. People are putting their wishes and desires in the cracks of the walls."

"But," added Patrick, "tell Linda what's happening to your regulars."

"It's true. Some of their wishes are materializing. A woman, a regular, she sees a handsome man, also a regular. She wishes to meet him. Puts that wish in the wall. Her next time here, she is seated next to him. There is no salt on her table. She must borrow his. The time after that, she is also seated next to him. Pretty soon they are coming in together. Another regular, a young man, an art student. He puts a note in the wall because he cannot get an appointment to show his work. Pretty soon he is seated next to the art dealer and her husband. There is talk of portfolios and an appointment is made."

"Very interesting. But is all this help coming from a higher power or from a Bedouin power?" I asked.

"This I cannot say." Habib had a guilty smirk on his face.

I inquired, "And if papers fall out of the wall late at night, uncrumble on their own, and you happen to be passing by ..."

"One cannot help seeing things in the path of one's vision, eh?" He turned to the young waiter, "Bring my friends some hummus and babaganoush." Then to us he added,

"Enjoy, I must go take care of business now." He disappeared into the kitchen.

"He must go work miracles now," I said to Patrick. Patrick steered the conversation towards my work. He was genuinely interested in my columns and wanted to discuss several of them. We had a delicious Middle Eastern lunch, and then he brought up the subject.

"Katherine suggested I help you with an affair." I was taken aback.

"What?"

"Your friend's wedding," he explained.

"My revenge date. Isn't it silly?"

"I can understand it. After all, didn't your husband walk out on you?"

"I can see Katherine tells you everything."

"I agree with Katherine that it would be more comfortable for you to attend with a friend," Patrick said.

"And you don't mind being a beard?" I asked.

"Actually, I'm a fan and could easily be a friend." Patrick was making it very easy for me. So I agreed to seriously consider taking him. He thought it would work better if we knew each other before Lillian's wedding, so I agreed to meet him later in the week to help him pick out a birthday gift for Katherine.

CHAPTER *Five*

I was worried about Drake. He was uncommunicative, even for him. I knew his father moving out must have had an impact. My girls seemed fine. Of course, Marv picked the kids up every weekend and saw them after school several times a week. They had plenty of phone conversations in between. But I knew a marriage breakup is toughest on the kids. I made an appointment to see a family therapist.

Dr. Burke's office was downstairs in the back of her house in Highland Park, one of the North Shore's tony suburbs. She had instructed me on the phone to just let myself in and wait in her office. I entered into a hallway. On the right was the living room. It was all blue and white like a piece of Wedgwood. The white carpeting had fresh vacuum tracks in the shape of decorative swirls to match the wallpaper. I thought it was unbelievably neat and clean and figured she could not have any children or pets.

On the left was a mirrored wall with a Post-It that read, *Come Downstairs.* I went downstairs and walked past a home gym. There, on a stationary bike, was a woman in slacks and a blazer with pouffy blonde hair as if she had just been to the beauty parlor. She seemed to be about seventy, and she was exercising in full makeup. "Hi, I'll be right there," she shouted to me. "Just go into the office."

I continued down the hall and saw the office. I went in and sat on the leather couch. The woman who had been exercising, who I now realized was Dr. Burke, came into the room, and sat across from me on a swivel desk chair.

"Linda, I'm Terri Burke. You can call me Terri." Her face was moist. "I like to workout between appointments. I can do that in my work clothes because I don't sweat."

I noticed she was hiding gum in her cheek. While we talked, she kept transporting her gum from one cheek to the other and sneaking a quick chew when she thought I wasn't looking. She seemed professional, other than the shvitzing and the chewing, so I opened up.

Terri was very familiar with the burden of children of Holocaust survivors. She had worked for the Jewish Council for the Elderly. I explained Marv was careful around the kids. He didn't want to have the same relationship with them that his parents had with him, especially the father-son relationship.

I explained how Marv had decided one day that we (he) weren't happy. He was approaching his fiftieth birthday and was thinking about the rest of his life. He couldn't waste any more of my time or his in an unhappy marriage. He would still provide for me and always be there for the kids, but he needed to get happy and that just wasn't happening.

I explained how Marv had a complicated relationship with his parents, aging Holocaust survivors. They were always disappointed in him. He could never live up to their expectations, and he had the burden of having to make up for all the family members they had lost.

After a brief overview of my family, we began discussing the kids. "My two teens are completely different. Drake is quiet, moody. He comes in the house and heads straight for his room. Agatha is talkative. She confides in me and loves to spend time with me."

"I understand your concern," Terri said while shifting gum hiding spots in her mouth, her tongue darting from east to west. "Of your two teens, one is not acting normal. This is troubling. Would you like me to have a session with her?"

"Her? You mean him."

"No. Drake is behaving like a typical teen. That's his way of rebelling. Adolescence is a time of rebellion. It is important that teens find a nondangerous way to rebel. Your daughter is not doing that. This is what concerns me — her excellent behavior. It's just not normal." She was playing gum ping-pong in her cheeks as she was explaining. I left Dr. Burke's home-office more confused than when I entered.

I was driving back to the city on Edens Expressway. The traffic was slowing down probably due to a gapers block somewhere or the constant highway construction. I was watching men and women in orange vests clearing away debris and garbage from the grassy embankments. I thought they might be convicts that sometimes do that sort of work. I heard the song *My Favorite Things*. I lowered my window. The probable prisoners were singing show tunes. I noticed a tall, good-looking man in an orange vest. He was picking up garbage and seemed to be leading the singer/prisoners. He looked familiar, and I realized he was an old friend of mine. I pulled over to the shoulder, parked my car, and walked toward him.

"Greg?" I questioned, although I was pretty sure it was him. He turned to me. Surprised, it took him a moment to place me. Then he grabbed me and hugged me.

"Linda, Darling."

"Greg, wha ..."

"No names dear." He shushed me.

"Are you a convict?" I whispered.

"Not quite," he whispered back. "Community service. I can't explain now. I have to get back to work. Can we meet later?" We made plans to meet that evening at a deli in Skokie.

I arrived at the deli, Barnum and Bagelah, before

Greg and was seated in a booth under a menacing-looking clown mask. All around the dining room were weird circus paraphernalia. The theme, a mixture of Emmett Kelly and smoked salmon, apparently appealed to the ninety-year-old set because the place could have doubled for an assisted living facility.

I was excited to see Greg. We had lost contact, and before this day, I hadn't seen him in several years. We had met over a quarter century ago when we were both taking improv classes at Second City. Greg was the star of the class. His talent seemed limitless. I was aware that over the years he had moved back and forth from Chicago to LA to New York performing in various shows, but as far as I knew, his big break never came. I saw Greg come in as tall and good-looking as ever, only now, he had salt and pepper hair.

"Darling." He sized up the surroundings, "What is this, an assisted eating facility?"

"I know. I thought you'd like the weirdness, and they have a bar," I informed him.

"I don't drink anymore, but you have something. Can we find a waitress or is there, perhaps, a nurse on duty."

Our waitress came over. Her name tag said *Ruby*. She took our orders—maztoh ball soup and a brisket sandwich for Greg—chicken noodle soup and a glass of merlot for me.

"Love Ruby's 'do," Greg commented when she walked away. Ruby, although in her sixties, had pitch-black dyed hair that she wore in a big, high bouffant. Her eyebrows were plucked off and then painted on with thick black liner. She wore deep red lipstick painted way over her natural lip line. Her polyester waitress uniform was two sizes too small. She wore dark hose and white nurse's shoes. I knew Greg would appreciate the kitschy atmosphere. It seemed the perfect environment for the story he was about to tell me.

I came back to Chicago six months ago. I had been doing this play in Santa Monica, *The Man in the Microfibre Dinner Jacket*—got great reviews. Thought I'd get some auditions from it but nothing happened. I was running out of money, so I sublet my apartment and came back here to stay at my folks' house. They spend the whole winter in Vegas anyway. I was still drinking then, and I started visiting one of *the boys bars*, Room Service. One night I'm hanging out at the bar, and this creep keeps trying to make contact. But I'm busy 'cause this big, Nordic-looking blond is giving me the eye. A couple of drinks later, me and the Viking are fooling around, making out in a corner, hands everywhere. This is all a blur, but when I left Room Service, the creep is right outside, and he handcuffs me—don't get too excited—it's not that kind of a story—he arrests me. This is in some podunk suburb, and they have some ordinance—licentious behavior. If a straight couple had been acting this way it would be legal. You would not believe what I had to go through. I had to find a lawyer. I'd go into these offices. The attorney would say something to me like, 'Don't worry whatever you've done—you can tell me. I've represented drug addicts, murderers,' then I'd explain, and the guy would practically retch right there. Murderers, rapists are okay, but fooling around with another guy, that makes him puke. Here's the worst part—if you get convicted of this you have to register as a sex offender. That meant I'd be listed online with the fifty-two-year-old perv who attacks twelve-year-olds. As if that's the same as two consensual men.

Greg further explained that he finally found a sympathetic attorney who was able to get his charges reduced to a misdemeanor. He wouldn't be blacklisted as a sex offender, but he'd have to do community service. He was so grateful that he decided to make the best of it and got all the other people doing service with him to perform showtunes and enjoy cleaning up the roads.

We had a great time catching up, and I was glad to reunite with him. We promised we'd keep in touch.

As we parted in the Barnum and Bagelah parking lot, Greg told me, "Next week I'll be on the Edens, between Lake Cook and Half Day Road. We'll be doing *Funny Girl*—you must stop by."

Chapter Six

*L*inda*." It was my friend Jen. "I have to make the plans for our summer getaway. It looks like it's going to be late July, if that's okay with you, 'cause Mitzi says she can't go in August, and Doree will go whenever we want. I don't think we can count on Lillian this year, and Caro told me we should just pick a weekend, and she'll see what she can do. I can't imagine Lillian would leave Barry – being a newlywed."*

"She always has some excuse. Maybe she'll drive up for a day," I said.

"I'm not counting on it. If we don't book now, everything will be filled. I'm going to put a hold on a suite at the Grand Geneva. Guess who Albert ran into?" Jen asked.

"Marv."

"How did you know?" She was surprised.

"Lately, whenever anyone says, 'Guess who I ran into,' it's always Marv. So, what did Marv have to say?"

"Oh, Albert didn't talk to him. He saw him at Maggiano's – across the room. He said Marv didn't see him.

Albert was just picking up a to-go order for me — shells and roasted vegetables, and Marv was with some woman, so Albert said he didn't want to embarrass him. I told Albert he definitely should have embarrassed him, but you know men. I asked him to describe the woman, but he didn't even bother to take a good look at her."

We agreed that late July would be the best time to plan our getaway, and that men are not nearly as talented at embarrassing others as women.

"Good Lord Linda." It was Katherine. She was standing next to my desk. "Why didn't you ... We can't talk here. Come into my office. You can pull yourself away from your carrel."

"Carrel." I hadn't heard that term since high school. "Why do they call cubbies carrels?" I asked.

"How the hell should I know. For that matter, why do they call them cubbies? Cubby, carrel, either way sounds like two of the Mouseketeers. Just follow me."

I followed her into her office. She closed the door. "Good Lord Linda, you're seeing Patrick today, and you didn't even tell me."

"It's no big deal. I'm just helping him shop," I said.

"I know. I'm sure he says it's for my birthday gift, but it's really to see you."

"A lot of men like help in picking out a gift for a woman," I insisted.

"Not Patrick. He has exquisite taste. Always gets me something beautiful, and he doesn't need help doing it. I gather he felt it was a good excuse to spend time with you."

"He thinks we should know each other better before showing up at Lillian's wedding. That makes sense. He's being helpful. I don't want it to seem like it's our first date when I run into Marv and his friend. But, I'm still not sure if I'm taking Patrick," I said.

"Do you know if Marv is serious with someone? Have there been Marv sightings?" Katherine asked.

"I have been getting reports of Marv and some woman in restaurants at Old Orchard Mall and once at the movies in Highland Park, but I can't be sure it's the same woman," I told her.

"I'm certainly glad you're seeing Patrick," she said. But was I *seeing Patrick*?

"Again, Katherine, I don't think we're *seeing* each other. He's helping me out, and I'm helping him out today shopping.

"Good Lord Linda, you are delightfully naive, but maybe that's one of the things Patrick adores about you." In Katherine's mind I was now *adored*.

"Adoration might be a slight exaggeration," I told her.

"You are an innocent."

"Look," I explained. "I really don't think Patrick has any interest in me other than he enjoys my column, but if he were to have an interest, I don't see a problem."

"I think you do. I think you're caught up in the age difference or something like that, but believe me, that sort of thing isn't important, so just enjoy yourself and," she was leading me out the door, "don't let him spend terribly too much money on my gift, even though he can well afford it." She shut the door behind me.

Entering the main office that housed the writer's cubbies, Sara, a small nondescript woman who wrote the obits, had witnessed this and approached me.

"What was that about?" she asked.

"Spending parameters on gift shopping."

"Oh," she shrugged and was off to the Xerox machine.

Patrick took me to lunch at the Walnut Room at Marshall Field's State Street Store. I knew Marshall Field's had been bought out by a large company, Federated, and that they usually change all the department store's they buy to Macy's.

"I don't care if they change all the store's names. I will never call Marshall Field *Macy's*. When Westfield bought Old

Orchard, I refused to call the mall anything but Old Orchard, and my readers did the same. For years we called that hotel in Lincolnwood, the Purple Hyatt, even when it was the Lincolnwood Radisson, we still only called it the Purple Hyatt. Finally they changed the name to the Purple Hotel."

"You really feel strongly about this?" he asked.

"It's plain old Midwestern stubbornness. Not being a native Chicagoan, you might not understand."

"We left New York when I was eighteen. I picked up on it. I've lived in Chicago a pretty long time." But how long, I wondered, trying to estimate his age.

"I don't even like when people change their names. I have a friend, Lawrence. He's a hairdresser. One day he announces that we should call him Martin because Martin is the Patron Saint of hairdressers. I'm not even sure I believe it. And my childhood friend Liz Brown marries a fellow named Bill Putzenberg. She actually takes the name Putzenberg. As if that weren't bad enough, a few years ago she tells me she always hated the name Liz and to call her Polly. Now whenever I tell my Mom that I'm getting together with Polly Putzenberg, she asks 'Who?' and I say, 'Liz Brown'."

So, I gather your ex's name isn't Grey," Patrick said.

"No, but I'm not against taking a spouse's name. I just didn't want to do it. I was already an established writer, and I like my name. But still, I think you should reject the notion of taking someone's name if it's Putzenberg or Schmendrake or something like that."

"I never liked having the same name as my father, grandfather, and great-grandfather. I would never do that to my son."

"It's very distinguished."

"You mean very *WASPISH*."

"There's nothing wrong with that," I told him, remembering in college how Caro and I had a fascination with the boys in the *WASPY* Fraternity house across the street. Caro would sound out their names as if it were poetry ... William Austin Smith the Third, Chad Covington Jr., Jeffrey Douglas Benninton the Second.

"That's just the problem," he said as he leaned towards me and opened his collar to reveal a gold Star of David on a chain resting against his curly blond chest hairs. I was stunned!

"But you're not Jewish." That was more a question than a statement.

"I am. My mother was Jewish, Rina Rosen Rainey. She died when I was nine, and my father married Katherine when I was seventeen. But I was always in contact with the Rosen side, especially when we still lived in New York. I consider myself Jewish but having my WASPY name throws most people off. You wouldn't believe some of the things people have said to me about Jews. Then I tell them that I'm Jewish. They get all flustered until, finally, they tell me how much they enjoyed *Fiddler On The Roof.*

While Patrick was explaining all this to me, I kept trying to get a peek at that Star of David resting on his chest hairs, but he had rebuttoned his collar. I imagined my retinas burning a hole through his cotton weave.

We headed over to the Maller's Building on Wabash and entered Jeweler's Row. Patrick took me up to the eighth floor where his friend had an office. Avi, Patrick's friend, greeted us and served us Turkish coffee. He had a nice sleek, modern office with a work room in the back. Avi disappeared into the back room and returned with a box.

"I think this came out just as you wanted." He handed the box to Patrick. Patrick opened it revealing a large silver pin that was a replica of the Northside News front page with small gem stones embedded into it to represent the news type.

"Avi, it's perfect. You captured my idea exactly!" Turning to me Patrick announced, "The man's absolutely brilliant. He's a real artist and can do anything."

"Katherine will love it," I said. I could just imagine how pleased she was going to be when she saw it, probably exclaiming, "Good Lord Patrick, you're a genius."

So Patrick didn't need anyone to help him pick out Katherine's gift. Maybe Katherine was right, and he was actually interested in me. Or maybe Katherine was imagining things, and I was a hopeless middle-aged woman whose husband had left her and was having a crisis. Whichever was the true answer didn't really matter. I was taking Patrick to Lillian's wedding. I didn't need an answer. What I needed was something fabulous to wear.

CHAPTER SEVEN

*G*reg *insisted on accompanying me on my quest for the perfect outfit. "We are not going to Loehmann's. I've been there with my sister. Everyone clawing in the communal dressing room. Once someone actually put on my sister's street clothes and wanted to buy them. No Darling. We'll find something and on sale."*

We tried the reduced racks at Nordstrom but nothing fit. Then we browsed through the sale racks at Lord and Taylor. We were at the Old Orchard Shopping Center, so we headed over to Saks Fifth Avenue. Greg picked several outfits off the reduced rack and had the sales lady bring them to me in the dressing room.

"It's so nice that your husband takes an interest in your clothes," commented Ruth, my sales lady.

"It is nice," I added. I knew Greg always liked being taken for straight, so I played along with it. Greg has always had great taste, so I wasn't surprised when I tried on a bright red raw silk Albert Nippon suit with a narrow long skirt. It fit me perfectly.

"Your husband wants you to model this one. I must say, it was made for you." Ruth looked at the price tag. "Wow, it's marked down sixty percent."

I modeled it out of the dressing room. Greg grabbed me and danced me around the dress racks. "You look perfect," Greg sang.

"I've never worn so much red."

"You should always wear red — with your complexion." He turned to Ruth, "You made a sale."

"I think you made the sale," was Ruth's reply.

We were eating a late lunch at Maggiano's. Greg ordered the pasta and roasted vegetables, which made me think of Jen's husband, Albert, running into Marv at this same restaurant. Albert had been picking up pasta and roasted vegetables when he spied Marv and his mysterious, descriptionless, dining partner. So many people I know come here. I wondered who might see me with Greg. But Greg could not be descriptionless — tall, good-looking, elegant, affectionate, witty — all the telltale signs that he's a gay friend instead of some romantic suitor. Still, Ruth the saleslady had been fooled. There I was eating my stuffed mushrooms and drinking a glass of chablis in the middle of the day hoping someone who knew Marv would walk into the dining room.

"They're absolutely beautiful, Darling." Greg was looking at pictures of my kids on my cell phone. "The baby looks like you. Drake is stunning. You'll have to watch out for the girls — and the boys. Agatha is gorgeous, a clone of Marv. I am sorry about Marv, darling. I always thought the two of you were a perfect match. He's so sweet. If I were straight, and a woman, I would go for him. So what was the problem?"

"That's what I never understood. He claims he wasn't happy. I don't know what he's searching for. We got along well, but he was moody.

"I never saw that, but it has been along time since I saw Marv."

"He never showed his moody side to anyone but me. He has all this family *mishugas*."

"The Holocaust stuff," he added knowingly. "Does his

brother still lead a double life?"

"Oh yeah. Stuey's been married for twelve years and has two kids. Marv's parents don't even know about it. They think he's living this single life in Milwaukee. You'd think they'd wonder why a forty-five-year-old man never married, but they assume he's a professional bachelor."

"Bachelor! That's so archaic. You mean like Clifton Webb or something?" Greg asked.

"I guess. My father-in-law goes insane at the thought of his sons dating a gentile, and here he has one married to a black woman and with kids."

"Couldn't she be one of those Ethiopian Jews?" Greg asked.

"From the south side of Chicago?"

"If your in-laws found out?"

"My father in-law claims, if anything like that ever happens, he's moving to Israel," I said.

"That couldn't help the peace process any," was Greg's reply. "So Marv's brother is basically living a lie."

"Basically," I agreed.

"Well, look who's in the closet, and this time, it's not me."

CHAPTER EIGHT

I had an outfit. I had someone to take. Now I just had to wait for Lillian's wedding. I was looking forward to seeing my old college friends. As it turned out, I would see them weeks before Lillian's nuptials. Caro had unexpectedly come in town from Park City to help clear out her father's house.

"He recently decided he wants to move into the Oak Park Arms. It's an assisted living facility in Oak Park, and most of his cronies live there. They play cards and *kibitz*. It'll be nice for him. But all those *chachkes* in the house, oh brother, I don't know how I'm ever going to unload all of that *chazarai!*"

We were at Starbucks on Touhy Avenue. And I knew exactly to what Caro was referring. Her Mom had passed away over a year earlier, and the woman was an eccentric who collected everything. Her walls were completely covered with framed valentines, postcards, and printers' drawers filled with miniatures. You name it. The woman collected, saved, framed, and displayed everything she could get her hands on. Every surface in that house was covered with Hummels, Lladros, china cups, antique dolls, and more. She even had a spare bedroom filled with paper maché clowns.

"My cousin Ben's daughter, Jessica, came by earlier. She just bought a condo downtown, and I had her take some china and flatware. And listen to this. She tells me Ben's upset because she's been seeing a married man for three years. She's twenty-six, and she tells me he's a lot older. He's a personal injury lawyer. Get this, she tells me he's really into tennis, and he's so hairy he shaves his body. She wouldn't divulge his last name, but she called him Marshall."

"Marshall Goldman! He was shaving in the sixth grade," I told her.

"Isn't Doree good friends with his wife Tess?"

"Yes. It has to be Marshall Goldman," I exclaimed.

We agreed we shouldn't tell anyone about Marshall's indiscretion with Caro's cousin's daughter and were back on the subject of unloading the contents of her family house.

"What about the antique dealers?" I suggested.

"I've got three coming over later, but there's as much crap as there is good stuff. Even after we get rid of the salable stuff, there'll be truckloads of junk to haul away. Dad says we should just torch it. He hates mom's collections. And that spare room, oh brother."

"The one that's a tribute to Emmett Kelly?" I interjected.

"That's the one. It just creeps him out."

"Maybe Barnum and Bagelah will buy that stuff," I suggested.

"That was Mom's favorite restaurant," Caro informed me. "Linda, it's wrong to leave so much crap for your kids to get rid of. I've gotten rid of all my old stuff. I don't want Jacob to have to deal with all my junk."

I was thinking about all the clutter I have in my house, especially Marv's stuff. He left all his podiatry books and foot journals with the horrible pictures of skin ulcerations. He promised he'd come get them, but he hadn't done it, and I was left with everything. Even when he lived in the house,

I begged him to let me recycle those journals. They were in piles all over the basement and living room. He thought he might need to reference them someday, but he wouldn't know where a specific journal was, and besides, with the internet, he could just download any article online. But he was attached to his clutter. The covers of those magazines had horrible photos of deep, oozing wounds.

I could just imagine the photographer who specializes in podiatric photography. I could see him showing his portfolio. "This is a gangrenous, club foot with displaced metatarsals. Notice the deep purple color and rich green," and his prospective clients, foot journal editors, reactions, "lovely, uh, oow, very nice indeed."

"You haven't told me about this guy you're bringing to the wedding," Caro said.

"Patrick Rainey the Fourth," I told her.

"I like that name—Patrick Rainey the Fourth," Caro seemed to be in a trance as she went on with more names. "William Riley Whitman the Third, Douglas George Shook Junior, Jeffrey Scott Hummel the Second." Caro was reminiscing about those frat boys across the street at the U of I. "William Robert Jennings Jr., Anthony Francis Pennington, David Greenberg."

"Right, the token Jew, and very cute. And, remember the night Jeffrey Scott Hummel the Second and Douglas George Shook Junior taught us to mix martinis?"

"Those were the days," she exclaimed smiling and sipping her grande decaf-caramel-machiato-soy-latte.

The next day Jen, Doree, and I stopped over at Caro's dad's house to help her box up some of the junk. It was a daunting task. Every surface was still covered with collections. Even the beds were covered with little china cups, salt and pepper shakers, and piles of paper. I have to admit, I rather enjoyed seeing how much stuff there was because I knew if Caro could get rid of all of that, maybe I could clean out my house. Suddenly, all my stuff didn't seem so overwhelming. We sat down in the kitchen, the only place where there was room to sit and the chairs weren't covered with stuff.

"I told Hilary and Hailey—when you finish college and law school you can always come back to live with us but don't bring any more stuff into the house," Jen said.

"I got rid of my crap the day I tossed Richard out." That was Doree referring to her ne'er-do-well ex-husband. He could never hold a job and didn't want to work, especially since he knew Doree had a big trust fund from her grandfather.

Caro's father walked in from the family room. I hadn't seen him in years. He was wearing a short-sleeved shirt and it appeared that he had no arms. I was shocked and surprised that Caro hadn't warned me. I knew he had health problems, but she hadn't mentioned that he had his arms amputated. Suddenly, he pulled his arms from behind his back. Since his shirt was short-sleeved, and his hands had been behind his back, it had only appeared as if he had no arms. He said hello and went back into the family room.

"What's with you?" Jen had noticed my reaction.

"I thought Caro's dad had no arms," I whispered.

"You're nuts!" Doree laughed.

"She's not so nuts. She's bringing some young stud to Lillian's wedding," Caro added.

"How old is this guy?" Doree asked.

"That's the problem. I have no idea."

"Why don't you just ask him?" suggested Jen.

"'Cause if you ask for that information, you have to be prepared to give out the same information on yourself," said Doree.

"Oh, I don't care about my age," I said.

"So ask Katherine," Caro suggested.

"I did. She won't tell me. Said it doesn't matter. She said he's basically in the same category as me."

"Maybe she means like those boxes you check off in market research surveys. You know, 35-50," said Jen.

"Maybe she means somewhere between The Olson Twins and Studs Terkel. You're both in that category," added Doree.

"Just ask him if he remembers where he was when Kennedy was shot," suggested Caro.

"He wasn't even born yet. Ask him where he was when Lennon was shot," said Jen.

"Lenin?" asked Doree.

"John Lennon," Jen clarified.

"Better play it safe. Ask him if he remembers where he was when Tupac Shakur was shot," suggested Doree.

We spent the next two hours wrapping little chachkes in newspaper and filling boxes. Everyone looked exhausted, and I could tell Caro found this overwhelming.

"We need a drink," I said.

Caro went over to a Victorian buffet that had rows of liquor bottles. She tried pouring an old bottle of Scotch into a shot glass but found the bottle was empty. She kept trying more bottles. They were all empty.

"This is just another collection. An empty bottle collection," Caro said. She looked like she was on the verge of tears.

"Can't we get a drink somewhere around here?" I asked.

"There's some old tavern around the corner in Forest Park. I've never been in it, but we can walk," said Caro. So the four of us walked over to O'Dooley's Pub.

"Jeez, who goes to a tavern in broad daylight?" asked Jen as we entered.

"A bunch of unemployed blue collar guys," was Doree's whispered reply as she looked around.

"And four middle-aged Jewish women looking to get *shikkur*," I added. The place was dark inside. It had a long curved wooden bar. Behind the bar was a pot-bellied, balding bartender with a thick mustache. Behind him was a color TV featuring sports on cable. It looked like a curling tournament. There were three men sitting at the bar ignoring the TV. I noticed a few tables with men drinking and hanging out together, and one table with an older bald gentleman accompanied by a woman in her sixties with long dyed blonde hair. She was pudgy and had on too much makeup even for a dimly-lit bar. Since it was still daylight outside, it took a few minutes for our eyes to adjust. Doree and I both walked into tables before we could see our way around. Jen felt her way to a four top and sat down. We all followed feeling our way over to the table.

"I don't see any waitresses," said Jen. "Maybe it's self-serve. What does everyone want?" Just then the bartender noticed us and yelled over the heads of the three men at the bar.

"What can I get you four beautiful young ladies?" he asked.

"I think he's been sampling his own product," Doree whispered. Jen and Doree ordered chablis. "I'll have a Jack Daniel's, neat," I said.

"I'll have that too," said Caro.

"Coming right up gorgeous," said the bartender.

The older blonde woman got up and headed towards the ladies room. I noticed she was wearing a short skirt and heels. Although she didn't have cankles, she didn't have the legs or figure for the skirt. Thinking how this poor, older woman was probably once young and beautiful depressed me. She might have had a great figure in her youth. But now, with her long, dyed blonde hair, she looked more like Mae West than a young beauty. By now, our drinks had been served. As I downed my shot of Jack Daniel's, I thought how difficult it must be for that woman to face the loss of youth. I wasn't even paying attention to my friends, and then without thinking I blurted out, "Time can be cruel."

"What?" Jen asked me.

"What?" I said.

"You just said something."

"No I didn't," I answered.

"You said 'Time can be cruel'," added Caro.

"I didn't say anything."

"I guess Alzheimer's can be cruel too," said Doree.

"I was just talking to myself."

"At least wear an earpiece and pretend you're on the phone," said Doree.

I noticed Mae West returning from the bathroom with a long piece of toilet paper hanging out from under her skirt. I felt tears starting to run down my cheeks.

"What's with you?" Doree asked.

"It must be the smoke," I said.

"Strangely enough," Doree said as she looked around, "no one is smoking."

"It's the Jack Daniel's," I told them.

"Yeah, Jack always does it to her," Doree said.

"I think we need another round," said Caro.

"I'll get it," offered Jen. She got up and went over to the bartender.

"I want each of you to pick out something from my mom's stuff," said Caro.

"But I'm trying to empty my house, not fill it," I said.

"Come on, there must be something you can use."

"Well, I don't have any nice water goblets," I said.

"Did you see the blue set or how about the cranberry glass?" asked Caro.

"Yes, I like the cranberry glass. My grandmother used to have a set like that. Okay, I'll take them. Thanks."

"Take some dolls for Delilah," Caro suggested.

"One, I'll only take one. I know she'd love them but there are way too many. Were all those dolls yours and Debbie's?" I asked.

"No, those were Mom's. But not from her childhood. She started collecting those about twenty years ago just after her clown period and before her spoon period," Caro explained.

I had forgotten about the spoon collection. She had a closet door in the master bedroom with dozens of collector spoons made of pewter with the names of different cities on them lined up and hanging all over the door. I wondered why anyone would want those spoons. They're not even functional. I started seeing the spoons dancing in my head with their different names attached to the handles ... Jersey City, Des Moines, Tallahassee, Peoria.

I was getting tipsy, so I made a conscious effort to pay attention to my friends. That's when Caro asked Doree, "How's your friend Tess?"

"She's great. I'm seeing her tomorrow," was Doree's reply.

"Doesn't she have twins?" Jen asked.

"Triplet preteens," Doree informed us.

"How's Marshall?" Jen inquired.

Caro and I exchanged knowing glances, and our eyes must have met for too long because Doree suddenly said, "What? What?"

"What?" said Jen.

"Not you, them," said Doree accusingly, referring to Caro and me.

"What?" said Caro.

"What?" I said trying to look innocent.

"You both know something. I saw you look at each other, and you held your gaze for about four seconds. That's three seconds too long. It means something," said Doree.

"It doesn't mean anything," I insisted.

"It means something," Doree reiterated.

"Linda's right. It doesn't mean anything. My girls do that all the time like when the discussion turns to sex, drugs, or spending too much money, so I know it doesn't mean anything," explained Jen.

Now we were all locking eyes with each other. Jen caught on. "Oh my God, it does mean something when they lock eyes. Hilary and Hailey told me it means nothing. But it doesn't mean nothing. It means something."

"Who says?" said Caro playing it cool.

"Doree just said it, and now you're all staring at each other like the opening sequence of *The Brady Bunch*," said Jen

"Yeah it means plenty," said Doree.

"We didn't say anything," Caro commented.

"That's just it," explained Doree, "less is more."

"Then nothing is everything," chimed in Jen.

"Exactly!" was Doree's reply.

"We need another round." Jen got up to go to the bar.

"I can't have any more," I said remembering all those collector spoons spinning in my head. "Just coffee."

Jen turned back to us, "Just don't tell what you know until I get back."

"You know ..." started Caro.

"We can't talk until Jen returns, and then, I want all the details," said Doree.

"What details?" I said.

"That's good, but when Jen gets back with the drinks, you're both talking," ordered Doree.

Caro started humming. "Lah-di-dah." The way the three of us kept looking at each other did feel like the opening credits of *The Brady Bunch*. Jen returned with our drinks. She passed them around.

Doree leaned in towards the center of the table and said, "A.P.—assume the position." We all leaned in towards the center of the table at the same time. Caro kept insisting she had nothing to tell but finally caved and repeated the story of her cousin's daughter to Jen and Doree.

"Caro, I can't believe you told. You're the one who said we shouldn't say anything," I said.

"In vino veritas," was her reply.

"Yeah, and in Jack Daniel's even more veritas and quicker," Doree added.

I started to imagine the story spreading around the North Shore. I really had nothing to do with it, but I felt bad for Doree's friend Tess. Then again, if she found out, it would be no one's fault but her husband's. Suddenly, the spoons started spinning in my mind.

"Jen, is this real coffee or decaf?" I asked.

"I think it's real. Real Irish coffee," she told me. But I didn't need anymore booze and neither did my friends who, I noticed, were getting sloshed. We couldn't handle the booze which is why I figured you rarely find a group of middle-aged Jewish women in an Irish pub in the middle of the day. Everyone looked buzzed, and Doree was finishing some story that I couldn't follow. She was slurring her words.

"I said to him. You can't talk like that to me, buddy. I'm a speech thathpologist." Everyone laughed.

"Now I've got a story to tell," said Jen. She proceeded

to tell us about her husband on the golf course. He was with three of his good friends. There was no one else near the hole they were playing.

"You better assume the position for this." We all leaned in as Jen instructed us. "Albert sharted."

"What?" asked Caro.

"Sharted," repeated Jen.

"He had too much confidence in a fart," explained Doree. "You know shit-fart."

Caro and I groaned out "Eww, ick," or words to that effect.

"Anyway, since no one was around except his good friends, he took off his underpants and left them, doody and all, on the course." Caro and I ceased being grossed out, and now we were howling with laughter. Jen went on, "So, when Albert gets halfway to the next hole, he hides behind a tree and looks to where he left his underpants. He sees the groundskeeper lifting it with a long stick, looking at his doody underpants."

We were all laughing so hard that we could barely catch our breath. "And here's the kicker. When Harry turned fifteen last year, he started wearing the same size as Albert, so I put labels in all their clothes, you know, so the housekeeper would know."

"But it just said *Albert*, right?" I asked.

"No. I already had a stack of labels for the dry cleaning clothes, so they don't get lost at the cleaners. That's what I had sewed on."

Doree said, "You mean the groundskeeper picked up Albert's doody underpants with a stick and read ..."

"*Albert Fishman Attorney at law*," added Jen. We all hooted and hollered.

We had all had too much to drink, and now we had to walk back to the house. We stopped in at a Starbucks. I didn't think a cup each would be enough, so I ordered one of their big to-go containers. It serves twelve, and we carried it back to Caro's family house. Jen poured out the coffee into some of the pretty china cups, but Caro had boxed up most of the flatware, so she went upstairs to the closet and came down with five pewter spoons. I was stirring my coffee with a spoon marked Portland.

"Can we even use these spoons?" I asked. "They might have lead in them."

"As long as you don't use them everyday. Don't worry," said Caro. We had to sober up before any of us could drive home, so we sat in the kitchen and started sharing stories of our kids. Caro told us how her son had left an instant-message on his desktop. It was between him and a female classmate. And this young girl was writing pretty sexy stuff.

"She was calling him sexy. And she wrote that she gets horny thinking of him."

"Can you be sure it was someone from school? They can meet strangers online," said Doree.

"I'm sure 'cause she wrote *I missed you in school today.* These young girls are really forward," said Caro.

"Well at least it's not from a stranger. But, did you ever consider it might have been a teacher?" Jen suggested.

"Oh, I doubt that. No one has given him a good enough grade to warrant talking like that. Any teacher that writes those things to Jacob had better give him an A, and that semester, he didn't get anything better than a C."

"Ah, a C ... the Jewish F," I added.

"Correct," Caro went on. "Anyway, I didn't know what to do. I showed it to Steve, but he said a stepfather really can't butt in. So, I left it alone, but I do check the caller ID on Jacob's cell phone when he leaves it home for charging."

Jen suggested "You really need to check the kids' phones, your husband's phone ..."

"And anyone else's you can get your hands on," added Doree.

"You might want to suggest that to your friend Tess," Caro said.

"I don't want to be responsible for the breakup of Tess's marriage," Doree said. "It's awful knowing someone's secret."

"Oh brother, I know a lot of secrets in Park City. It's such a small community. Steve never lets me have more than one drink when we're out with people," Caro told us. "Doesn't Marv's brother have a secret?"

"His folks still think he lives alone in Milwaukee. He told them there's a waiting list for landlines in Wisconsin, so they can only reach him on his cell phone. And he told them it's too long a ride for them, so he drives into Chicago to visit them."

"Doesn't Allen's brother have a similar situation?" asked Doree.

Allen, who is Mitzi's husband, is also the child of Holocaust survivors, so Mitzi and I are forever comparing notes.

"Allen's brother Peter has the opposite situation. He and his wife got divorced four years ago, and he hasn't told his parents. He's sure it would kill them, so everyone tiptoes around it. His ex-wife and his son go along with it for some reason. Crazy secrets," I said.

"I saw his brother's profile on J-date. It didn't say, *I'm in a pretend marriage*," Doree told us.

"Are you listed on J-date?" Caro asked Doree. J-date is a national Jewish online dating service, and every unmarried Jewish person I knew had registered on it.

"I am but I haven't met anyone. All the men our age want to meet women in their thirties," Doree said.

"I don't think it's all the men. Let's look at your profile," I suggested.

So Caro got her laptop from her pile of belongings in the corner of the living room and brought it back to the kitchen table. She hooked it up to the phone line, and Doree got it to her J-date profile. We all read it.

"Oh brother, no wonder no one's writing you," said Caro. "You have to sell yourself."

"I am of average height and weight with medium brown frizzy hair," I read aloud. "Are you kidding me?"

"Let's rewrite it. Change that line to ... I have a darling figure and luscious, curly chestnut hair," said Caro.

"She needs a new photo," Jen said to Caro and me.

"Hey, guys, I'm right here," was Doree's reply. But we were all ignoring her now. We were on a mission. We decided she needed an extreme makeover for her photo. Caro, Jen and I emptied the contents of our makeup bags and dumped it in the center of the coffee table.

"We should give her a facial first," suggested Jen. "Do you have any facial-mask here," she asked Caro.

"No, Mom never collected those," was Caro's answer.

"I know a great recipe for a facial. I wrote an article about kitchen cosmetics. We need an egg and coffee grounds."

"I don't have any coffee grounds," said Caro.

"I'll run over to Starbucks. I'm sure they'll give us some for a facial emergency," said Jen and she headed out the door. Caro and I sat in front of her laptop working on Doree's rewrite. We took turns typing and pushing Doree out of the way.

"Ooh that's good," I said reading Caro's input. "Change *somewhat* to *very.*"

"Very what?" asked Doree. She kept walking back to us to view the screen, but Caro just pushed her away.

"Go pick out something to keep. The Rosenthal dessert dishes are nice," said Caro.

"Take a paper maché clown home," I suggested.

"They are all the rage in Highland Park," said Doree straining her neck to see what we were writing.

"I think we should read some of the profiles," I suggested. Caro agreed, and she started looking up men in the proper age category.

"I like pretzels and other baked snacks," I read from a profile.

"Oh brother," commented Caro. "Well, you can't date him on Pesach."

Jen came back with the coffee grounds. "Here, they said they give them away all the time. People mix them in their potting soil. What can we do with her hair?"

"I'm right here guys," said Doree.

"I've got some product in my gym bag." I went out to the car to get the Murray's AfroGel.

I mixed enough coffee and egg mixture for all of us. We all sat there with grounds drying on our faces. We could hardly move our mouths when we talked. We had to purse our lips to speak because the egg was tightening so fast.

"I can feel my pores closing up," said Doree.

"That's good," I said. "You'll see, it's a really good facial."

"I had a glycolic peel last month," said Caro.

"You're always getting new procedures," said Doree.

"She's doing PR for a plastic surgeon," I said.

"Yeah, I don't pay for any of it. I couldn't afford it."

"I noticed your forehead hasn't moved since last year," I said.

"Botox, isn't it great?" Caro asked "I have to keep my looks. I'm in the public eye."

"Yeah," added Doree. "You have to keep your high profile high."

"Sounds like a good title for a novel. *Keep Your High Profile High*. You always wanted to write a novel," Caro said looking at me.

"Yeah, maybe when the kids are grown," I said.

"Delilah's five. You're going to wait another fifteen years?" Doree asked.

"We've been out of college like twenty-seven years," Jen said.

"Now you're depressing me," said Caro.

"Hey, time is standing still for you and your Botox."

"Well, let's see if we've improved any with coffee and egg," I suggested.

We rinsed off our facials and examined each others skin. Everyone agreed it was a good facial.

"Now that you're kitchen fresh, let's get started," I suggested.

"First some under eye cream or is this throat cream?" I pulled the tube as far from my face as my arms could stretch, but I still couldn't read the print. "I think it's for the eyes." I started applying it to Doree's eyes.

"Hey, that burns," said Doree.

"Let me see that," said Jen as she pulled the tube out of my hand. She took her glasses case out of her very organized purse, put them on, then read the tube. "For the throat. Avoid the nasal and eye area." Jen wet a paper towel and handed it to Doree who put it to her eyes.

"Jeez, Linda, get yourself some readers. That burns," said Doree.

After the stinging subsided, Caro applied moisturizer to Doree's face. Caro wanted to make-up Doree's face but so did Jen.

"I'm great with makeup. I grew up with Bobbi Brown," said Jen pleading her case.

"Great, so I'll have black eyes," commented Doree.

"Not that Bobby Brown, Bobbi Brown the cosmetics magnate. She's from New Trier."

"Well, I used to know Max Factor," said Caro. "Not the cosmetic's king. He was our *shul* janitor. He wasn't really Max. He was Maishie Factor."

"You can share my face," offered Doree.

"I still think the real Bobbi Brown beats a Maishie Factor," said Jen.

I started working on Doree's hair while Caro and Jen applied makeup.

"I wish you had some blonde highlights," I said.

"Sorry, it's mousy-brown with grey highlights," Doree responded.

"I've got an idea," Caro announced, and she started searching through her briefcase. She handed me a yellow highlighter marker.

Doree said, "You are kidding?"

"It's worth a try," I said and started highlighting Doree's grey hairs with the yellow marker.

"Don't worry, it'll look better in the photo." I finished her hair, and we all stood back to look at Doree.

Caro brought down a beautiful kimono from her mother's Asian collection for Doree to wear, and we posed her in the kitchen. We looked her over.

"The eyebrows need work," said Caro.

"Give me some tweezers," I said. Caro opened a drawer filled with tweezers and handed me a pair. I was leaning over Doree and squinting.

"Quick, someone hand Linda some glasses," pleaded Doree.

Caro gave me a pair with very thick lenses that were laying by the sink. "These are my dad's." I put them on and started to tweeze Doree's brows.

"Your dad is blind," I said.

"Can you see her eyebrow hairs?" Caro asked.

"I can see her DNA." I tweezed her brows. Doree now had two perfectly arched eyebrows. She looked great.

After much coaxing, we got Doree to pose with several attitudes: coy, seductive, flirtatious, serene, sexy, defiant, exuberant, pensive, and surprised. Caro took the photos with her digital camera; then we all looked them over.

"Which pose was this?" Jen asked.

"That was *surprised*," answered Doree.

"I think that was *disturbed*," said Caro.

"I didn't do *disturbed*," said Doree.

"Really, 'cause you look disturbed," said Caro.

"We're not going to use *disturbed* or *surprised*," I said. "How about this one?"

"That was coy," said Jen. "I like it."

"But that's not me," said Doree.

"She's right, better use *defiant*," I suggested.

We all agreed defiant was the best pose. Caro imported the photo of Doree, looking defiant, onto the computer and then uploaded it to Doree's profile page on the J-Date website.

"Oh brother, Doree, there you go into the ethernet," said Caro.

"You mean the internet," corrected Jen.

Caro responded, "Ethernet, internet ..."

"Ether way, I'm out there," said Doree. "Let's just hope I get a response before menopause sets in."

"Why, are you close?" asked Jen.

"We're all close," said Caro.

"I get my period every month," announced Jen.

"That's 'cause you're taking hormones," I said.

"I'm only taking them because I wasn't getting my period every month," Jen said.

"That is menopause," said Doree. "I'm regular. I was just at the doctor's for my yearly check-up. I told her I can even feel when I'm ovulating and she said, 'Oh, do you have *mittelschmerz*?' I told her 'I have mittelschmerz, *weltschmerz* and Ethel Schmertz'."

"What the hell is weltschmerz?" asked Caro.

I started to explain "It means world pain. It's when you have empathy for all the unfortunates in the world like the poor, the hungry…"

Doree added, "The lonely …"

Caro jumped in, "The overweight, the wrinkled."

"That's right," added Doree, "the unfortunate with fat asses and bad skin."

"In Park City, people with those problems are pitied," explained Caro.

"Well here in the Midwest, those conditions are de rigueur," Doree told us.

Caro's laptop was making noise. "Look," Jen was talking to Caro and me. "She's getting replies." We all looked at the computer.

"I'm right here, guys," Doree said but we ignored her.

"Maybe she'll get a date," said Jen.

"Maybe she'll get a boyfriend," added Caro excitedly.

"Maybe she'll get laid," added Doree under her breath.

CHAPTER NINE

*I*t's *wonderful that you have such close friends from college,"* Patrick said as he dipped a piece of pita bread into a plate of babaganoush. We were back at the Cafe Kotel. My article on the cafe had been published a few days before, and Habib had personally called me and requested that Patrick and I come for lunch. The place was packed. I noticed there now were small notepads and pencils on every table. The clientele were busy eating, talking, and writing. Patrick continued, "I have two friends that I've known probably for as long. It's just great when we three get together."

"If you've known your friends for the length of time that I've known my college friends, then the three of you must have met in the hospital nursery," I commented.

"That's very cute. But actually Linda, if you want to know my age all you have to do is ask me. Or, you could always do a Google search."

Of course, that kind of information is readily available on the internet. I don't know why I hadn't thought of it before.

"Have you already done that on me?" I asked.

"What? Looked up your age? No. I've told you I'm not interested in numbers," Patrick told me.

"Like the *Fourth*?" I said.

"Correct. Look Linda," Patrick grabbed my hand across the table, "age means nothing to me. You're the same woman you were at thirty-five only smarter, wiser, more interesting, and I imagine, just as attractive, if not more so." He was looking into my eyes, and I was thinking, if I could bottle that attitude and sell it, I'd be one of the richest women in town. I'd probably be richer than Oprah or Dipti. Patrick was unique. After all, according to Doree and other women I knew who had been single for a long time, most men wanted women much younger than them.

The next thing I knew, Patrick was giving out the dreaded information as if it was a cologne sample, he was a Calvin Klein rep, and I was an innocent shopper strolling through the cosmetics department at Lord and Taylor. "I'm thirty-nine." He sprayed the number directly into my eyes. It had a hint of cinnamon with a second note of musk.

"You're kidding." I was surprised.

"You look disappointed. Did you think I was older?" he asked.

"Actually, I thought you were about thirty-one," I admitted.

"So, you should be relieved, but I still sense you're disappointed," Patrick said.

"No, I'm just surprised, but I shouldn't be. Katherine said we were in the same category."

"Oh, market research, 35-50," Patrick said. Just then I saw Doree enter the cafe. I noticed she had tried to recreate the make-up and hair we had done on her for her J-Date photo. She hadn't quite achieved the same look, but it was close, and she looked good. She saw me and walked over to our table. I caught her eyes looking at my hand in Patrick's. I introduced her to Patrick. Doree explained that she was meeting a man from J-Date for lunch.

"Look what you've done for my business." That was

Habib who seemed to sneak up on us. I sensed he spotted us holding hands. He introduced himself to Doree. "Will you be joining us for lunch?" Habib asked Doree as he pulled out a chair for her.

"Not here. I mean not at this table. I'm meeting someone for lunch. Oh, I think that's him over there." Doree said her goodbyes and walked over to a table near the door where a middle-aged, average-looking fellow greeted her.

"Your friend seems charming. Attractive, with a defiant look I appreciate. Bring her back anytime." Habib called over to a young waitress, "Bring my friends the special appetizers," and he disappeared into the kitchen.

"Your article was wonderful. Look at the power of your words. People are waiting in line outside in forty degree weather," Patrick told me. We talked while Noa, the waitress, kept bringing us different Middle Eastern specialties. Patrick held my hand between courses, and the conversation meandered it's way to the subject of my writing a novel.

"I'm a terrible procrastinator," I said.

"On the contrary, a terrible procrastinator is no good at procrastinating. It sounds like you're a great procrastinator. You've been putting this off for years. You've perfected procrastinating. Now it's time to do what you've been putting off," Patrick told me.

"I don't think I have the ability to concentrate on something as big as a book right now," I said. Just then I noticed Doree's date walking towards the restrooms. I saw Doree seated at her table writing on a scrap of paper. She shoved the scrap into a crack in the wall. Habib went over to her. They seemed to be having a nice conversation and were both laughing.

"I see what you mean about your poor attention span," Patrick commented.

"What?"

"We're discussing your career, and you're concentrating on Doree's table. By the way, what is happening over there?" he asked.

"I don't know. Doree and Habib are laughing it up

while her date is in the men's room. Oh, here he comes." Her date was returning to the table. Now Habib was talking to both of them. Habib and Doree's date shook hands. Habib went over to a table of four men in navy blazers with pale blue shirts and similar ties. They all looked alike, and I took them for businessmen who never vary their wardrobe. While the men were talking to Habib, one of them inconspicuously shoved a note into the wall. Maybe he was wishing for some clothing that would differentiate him from his coworkers.

"I'm really looking forward to this wedding," Patrick told me as we stood outside the Northside News building. He had walked me back after our lunch at Habib's cafe.

"You don't even know Lillian."

"I know," he said, "but I want to meet your friends and see you in your element." An awkward wedding where my husband would show up with a woman was Patrick's idea of *my element*. Still, I knew this was a compliment. "I'd also like to see you in the evening," he added.

"Better lighting," I said.

"An evening date — when you don't have to run back to the office." I had been avoiding seeing him at night. That would seem more like dating, plus, he would meet my kids and that would seem like a relationship that might blossom. Daytime meetings felt more like we were just friends or business associates.

"So, you'll get started on your project?" Patrick was referring to my novel writing. I had agreed earlier, over mint tea, that I would begin writing. I couldn't think about it at the moment, because our usual Chicago winds kicked up, and the forty degree weather began to feel like thirty degrees. I could see people were having difficulty walking down Lincoln Avenue against the March winds. Sara, our newspaper's nondescript obit writer, was heading back to the building carrying a large bag I recognized from Kostas' Gyro Hut, a favorite lunch take-out place for our office. It appeared Sara had been designated pick-up person for that day. She was heading towards us when Patrick said, "It's settled, you'll stop procrastinating and I'll stop procrastinating. I'll stop this very minute, because there's something I've been putting off."

He grabbed me and planted a big, wet one—deep and passionate—smack on my lips. I felt dizzy, and I could smell the aroma of roasted lamb, garlic and onions. Patrick let me go after a very decent amount of time, said goodbye, and seemed to disappear. Meanwhile, the aroma got stronger, and I noticed Sara staring at me her mouth open; she had a dazed look in her eyes. The bag of gyros was split open on the pavement by her feet. She was standing in a pool of meat and yogurt sauce.

Answering e-mail in my cubicle, I was aware that someone was standing behind me. I turned around to find Katherine looking down at me with a knowing look in her eyes. She jerked her head towards her office, and I followed her inside. She shut the door. She was wearing a stunning, pink brocade jacket with the pin Patrick had given her for her birthday over her right breast.

"Good Lord Linda, Sara reeks of garlic, my staff is going hungry, and do you know why?" Katherine asked me.

"The poor quality of the paper bags Kostas packs his to-go orders in?" I answered.

"That is correct. If Kostas used a better quality paper bag it might not split apart when an innocent staff member sees you getting groped on the street."

"Aren't you overreacting?" I asked.

"Sara didn't even know you and Marv had split up."

"Since I'm feeling healthy, I thought it was premature to give any personal information to the obituary writer," I told her.

"But a perfect stranger?"

"Now Patrick's a stranger?" I asked

"Good Lord. I didn't know it was Patrick. That's different. Of course, Sara doesn't know Patrick. That's not groping. It must have been a gentlemanly kiss goodbye," Katherine decided.

"Patrick is most definitely a gentleman. You should be proud," I told her.

"I can't take too much of the credit. After all, Patrick was half grown by the time I got a hold of him. Rina and Paddy had already laid the groundwork. I just hope you don't hurt him."

"What?"

"Well," she explained, "if you're kissing him ..."

"He kissed me."

"Whatever, and if you and Marv get back together ..." Katherine said.

"Who mentioned anything about that?" I asked.

"Your divorce is dragging. Marv's bound to come around to his senses. He is a great guy." I had almost forgotten how everyone loved Marv, especially before our breakup. He was the Jewish answer to Ray Romano.

Maybe Marv was having a temporary midlife crisis and would want to get back together. After all, what had he really done? He had been a good father and husband. Maybe too critical. I hadn't noticed so much until he left. Then there was no one telling me I had stacked the dishwasher improperly or put his sport coats on the wrong hangers. I did feel a little lighter in my step. Although I was hurt by his leaving, I certainly wasn't miserable at home without him. I didn't miss hearing what I had done wrong around the house. Not that he was constantly critical. He was mostly critical when we were expecting company, especially his family. His father would be constantly criticizing our home and Marv's decisions. So naturally, Marv would be on edge whenever his folks stopped by.

There was the good side of Marv: funny Marv, sweet Marv, generous Marv, helpful Marv. The kids adored him, his patients adored him, the mailman adored him.

Somehow, I felt it wasn't me who Marv had walked out on—it was himself. I could no more try to figure out how to get him back than I could figure out how to get the wind to stop blowing or to get the sun to come out. Things happened, changed. I could only be an observer not a catalyst.

"I know Patrick. He doesn't just kiss someone lightly," Katherine went on. "And no jokes about him kissing you firmly. You know what I mean. I'm just concerned for him. If things don't work out, what will he have? At least Paddy has his maps, but Patrick puts everything into his relationships." I tried to imagine what Katherine's husband would do if she left him. I could see him having a glass of champagne and caressing his mariner's maps. Other than friendship, Patrick and I hardly had a relationship. What was Katherine worried about? Marv and I hadn't seen each other. He would pick up the kids when I wasn't home and drop them off in front of the house. And, there was a mysterious woman or possibly several that he was seeing. And, then again, there was Patrick's kiss. I was still thinking about that kiss, reliving it in my mind, when I noticed I was being led out of the room by Katherine.

"I guess I'm just an overprotective stepmother, so I know you'll be kind to Patrick, because I'm not only your friend but also your boss." And with that, I was back in the hall, and Katherine was in her office with the door shut.

Sara, who I noticed had cleaned herself up, came over to me and asked, "What was that about?"

"Just some new policy regarding wearing Greek food-scented cologne to work."

The next night I dreamt I was drowning in a sea of yogurt sauce. I kept trying to swim to shore, but the sauce was too thick. I was stuck in the middle of nowhere. Little fish were swimming past me, and they all had the face of Sara from the office. I was struggling to keep my head above water and kept thinking of my kids. I knew I needed to survive for them. I heard a boat horn and saw a large ship come into view.

I read the name, *USS Rainey IV*. Someone from the ship threw me a lifesaver, but when it hit the yogurt sauce, it turned into a notepad and pencil. Someone on the ship yelled through a bullhorn, "Write for your life." I couldn't swim and write. I was panicking. Just then I saw Marv in a row boat. He stuck his leg out and told me to grab onto his foot. I tried to grab it, but the Sara fish kept getting in my way. I heard the sound of bells and saw a shark with bells on it's fin aiming right at me.

The shark was wearing Katherine's pin on its side. The precious stones were falling out into the water. When the shark picked it's head out of the water, I could see it had Katherine's face. The Katherine-shark was coming closer, and the bells were getting louder. I woke up, but the bells were still ringing. It was my alarm clock. I had to begin my daily mad rush to get the kids off to school on time.

Chapter Ten

By nine o'clock I had everyone in school. Mitzi called to tell me she was in town for the wedding. We made plans to meet at Barnes and Noble in Old Orchard. I got there early and headed to the writing resources section. I grabbed a couple of books on novel writing and sat in the cafe to wait.

One book professed the merit of joining writing groups. But I had done that years ago, and it seemed like just a way to avoid writing by meeting with people to discuss writing. One book recommended attending writer's conferences. That seemed like a good idea if you already had a manuscript, because you could network with publishers, but again, you needed the manuscript. There was no way out of it. Attending workshops is not writing. Going to conferences is not writing. Taking classes is not writing. And reading books about writing is not writing.

I decided the only way to write a novel is to write, and so I began jotting down notes in the small notebook I always carry in my purse. I was excited, because the germ of a story was sprouting in my imagination. I began watering it, and soon characters began appearing as buds on a new branch. When I looked up from my notebook I realized something was going on in the cafe.

A young woman, most likely a college student, was sitting at a table near the window. She had shoulder-length, mousy-brown, flyaway hair. She looked upset as she discussed something with a Skokie police officer. I hadn't noticed the cop come into the cafe, but now I saw one of the Old Orchard — or should I say Westfield Shoppingtown (I refuse to call it that no matter how many signs they put up) — security guards joining them. I was straining to hear what was going on without looking like I was eavesdropping. But I didn't have to because the mousy-haired girl looked right at me and asked, "Did you see him?"

"See who?" I inquired.

"The fellow who exposed himself. He was just outside the window. His pants were open. Did you ever see anything like that?" she asked.

I didn't know how to answer that question. After all, was she inquiring whether I had ever seen anything like *that*, meaning a man's privates, or had I ever seen anything similar to a man's privates? Well, I remember getting a candle that looked like that from my pledge mom at AEPhi. Or, was she asking had I ever seen a flasher. I was trying to figure out whether I should answer her or if it was just a rhetorical question, when another man joined the cop and security guard. This man appeared to be a Barnes and Noble security guard. I never realized they existed. The nonplused coed kept asking people at neighboring tables if they had witnessed the incident. It seems no one else had had the privilege.

The girl was miming what the flasher did, and the Skokie cop asked her if the perpetrator had any distinguishing features. *Yeah, his schmuck was hanging out*, I thought she might say, but she didn't. She said she hadn't noticed. I could understand that. When someone is wearing an ostentatious gaudy piece of jewelry, you never seem to notice anything else about them. The two security guards and the cop were trying to figure out how to catch the perpetrator, but with no distinguishing features, they had nothing to go on. Except, maybe they should be on the lookout for a man running around Old Orchard tripping over his pants that are bunched around his ankles.

Mitzi arrived just then and joined me at the table. I explained to her what had been going on. "The poor kid," Mitzi commented. "Those pervs always approach the young girls."

"Of course," I said. "They figure they can't get a—you should pardon the expression—rise out of women our age," I said.

"They flash a young girl; she gets all flustered. They flash us; we look and say, 'Is that the best you got?'" Mitzi and I decided the flashers certainly weren't in it for the demeaning comments. "And there's no money in it," Mitzi said.

"It's not like they're flashing at the airport and have a jar for tips next to them," I said.

"No, they have to love their work. They do it for the reactions," Mitzi said.

"Yeah, reactions from young girls. Let's face it, Mitz, sadly, we're passed our getting flashed at prime," I said.

"Then let's at least eat something. What's good here?"

"I like the three-cheese grilled sandwich, and the desserts are yummy," I told Mitzi. We got some coffee, the grilled cheese sandwich, and a slice of chocolate layer cake to share.

"Who's doing the ceremony?" Mitzi asked.

"I don't know."

"Lillian's family is active in that super reform temple downtown," Mitzi told me.

"Oh, yeah. I once mentioned I thought it was low reform, and Lillian corrected me and told me it is classical reform. Did you know their Shabbos is on Sunday?"

"I think they serve challah at their seder," Mitzi added

"Oh come on?"

"Really. I was once there for a Bar Mitzvah, and I think they served bacon at the kiddush," Mitzi told me.

"Are you sure you weren't at a confirmation at an Episcopalian church?" I asked.

"I guess I might be thinking of one of those. It's getting hard to remember," Mitzi admitted.

"I can never remember where I parked my car. I'm always wandering around the parking lot with the remote pressing the alarm button."

"It's terrible. Sometimes I'm driving somewhere that I go all the time, and for some strange reason, I accidentally take a wrong turn. I worry about Alzheimer's," admitted Mitzi.

"It's not Alzheimer's. It's Some-Timer's, but it's not a disease. I wrote an article about it. We have too much to remember. Our brains are like computers, and there's only so much memory. When you use it up, it gets more difficult to retrieve the right information," I told her.

That's when the woman seated behind Mitzi turned around. She was about seventy, petite with salt and pepper hair, pleasant-looking, and well-dressed. She looked like someone's cute grandmother. The woman was alone at her table and had apparently been listening to our conversation.

"You need to keep your mind occupied. I'm doing crossword puzzles." She showed us her book of crossword puzzles. "Do anything you can to challenge yourself. Try something new. I tell my friends this all the time. You two are still young. You can do anything."

She got up, grabbed her purse, book of crossword puzzles, and left. It almost felt as if she wasn't real, like it had been a dream. Mitzi and I sat there for a minute without speaking.

Mitzi looked at me and said, "I'd love to learn to ice skate."

"I didn't know you can't skate," I said.

"I can go around the rink, but I mean really skate, figure skate ... twirls, twists, turns, leaps."

"It's not like you can't find a rink in Minnesota," I said.

"Oh, I can find a rink. I can find a teacher. I need to

find the time. And I know what Allen will say, 'How come you could skate today, but you didn't have time to press my shirt?'"

"Are you the only Jewish woman in the world who irons her husband's shirts?" I asked. I knew Mitzi did Allen's shirts and always thought she was nuts for not sending them out.

"I kind of enjoy ironing. It's relaxing. But Allen doesn't understand all I do. He just sees me as a part-time worker. He's been talking about how now that the kids are older, I can go to teaching full-time, like teaching part-time and being a full-time housewife doesn't equal one whole job.

"Women's liberation ruined it for us. A generation ago, if a woman stayed home to take care of three kids that was considered a big job—which it is. If she also worked part-time, well then, she was a hero. Now it's, 'when are you going to work full time?'" I said.

I remembered Marv used to ask me what I did all day, as if I did nothing, especially when I was writing articles from home. He just assumed the clothes cleaned themselves, the dry cleaning elves delivered his suits, and the kids never made a mess while he was out. When the kids were very little, trying to clean up after them was like mopping up during a flood.

Mitzi was on the subject of her once-a-week housekeeper. "It's not like she doesn't do a great job, but, and I'm not exaggerating, an hour after she's left, the whole house is a wreck again."

"You are exaggerating 'cause the house is a mess fifteen minutes later," I corrected her. "I know, because when Eugenia comes, that's how long it stays clean."

"I guess I could have Maudzilla come one more day," Mitzi said.

"Your housekeeper's name is Maudzilla?"

"I know. It's an unusual name."

"Is she thirty feet tall and hails from Tokyo?" I asked.

"I always think she should be a giant version of Beatrice Arthur. Actually, she's a lovely black woman from Georgia,"

Mitzi explained.

"Who's a lovely black woman from Georgia?" I heard a third voice ask. Mitzi and I looked up to see Caro standing above us.

"Caro," we both exclaimed.

"I called your mom's house. She told me you were both here," Caro said to Mitzi. She grabbed a seat and joined us. Caro explained she had arrived in town the night before and packed up more of her mom's stuff to donate to charity. She needed to take a break and decided to find us.

"I ran out last night to get more of those big plastic bins for packing. And, by the way, they're on sale at Target if you need any. I've got some buyers coming to see the house Sunday. Now that I took down all those framed cards, the walls look terrible. They're all cracked and peeling. But what can I do? I have to get back to Park City. My clients depend on me, and I'm due for another restilyn injection right here." She pointed to her laugh lines.

"Don't say too much. Linda has her notebook out, and she's writing a book," Mitzi warned Caro.

"Oh brother, not about us?" asked Caro.

"No. It's fiction, not science fiction. Actually, it's about a woman who is the child of Holocaust survivors and how that affects her life," I explained.

"You should talk to Allen. He has plenty of material for you," Mitzi suggested.

"I do plan to interview him," I told her. "The main character, Fran, has to tiptoe around her parents. They're very controlling, and she and her gay brother are afraid to injure them further, so they have to keep the brother's sexuality a secret. Basically, their whole lives are controlled by their aging parents' past."

"Wow, sounds heavy," commented Caro.

"It's really pretty funny, the way they always try to cover up stuff," I told them.

"I can see that. You should hear some of the lies we have to tell to keep my in-laws from finding out about Peter's divorce. They think Marsha is involved in hundreds of organizations and can never attend any family event, because she's chairing some meeting," Mitzi said. "Allen and Peter had to make up for everything their parents lost in the war. It's a huge burden. The Nazi terror did not end with liberation. Holocaust post-traumatic-stress syndrome is the gift that keeps on giving."

"So, the parents become the children and the children become the parents?" asked Caro.

"That's a good point," I commented and made some notes to include that theme in my story. "I need a refill. Anyone want some coffee?"

Caro said she'd have a tall caramel-half-decaf-soy-latte, so I left them at the table and went to the counter to order. While I was standing there, Sue entered the cafe. I could see Caro wave her over.

Sue sat down and joined them. They leaned close, *assumed the position,* and appeared to speak in whispers. They quickly pulled apart when I returned with the drinks. Sue explained she had been looking at magazines when she saw Caro and Mitzi. But now, she had to get some gifts at Nordstrom, and left.

"I haven't seen her in years. She looks great. How come we were never friends with Sue?" Mitzi asked.

"I don't know why *you* weren't. Of course, you didn't live at Bromley Hall, but Caro and Sue always liked the same guys. I think that came between you two," I said looking at Caro.

"I think that did. Especially Billy Berman. We both dated him at the same time. Too bad, 'cause Billy is a jerk and I like Sue," Caro admitted.

"What were the three of you talking about?" I asked.

"Oh nothing. Just life," said Mitzi, but I noticed my two friends' eyes met just a few seconds too long, and I wondered if they were discussing my marriage and/or divorce. I could tell they were hiding something from me, because Mitzi immediately changed the subject.

"The hood has really changed?" She commented. We call West Rogers Park where I live the *hood*. Mitzi grew up there, and her mom still lives in her old Tudor house on Lunt Avenue. I grew up in nearby Skokie, but when I married Marv, he already owned the Chicago bungalow, so I moved in and we stayed. Over the years the neighborhood changed from being mostly secular Jews to being mostly ultra-orthodox Jews and that's the change that Mitzi was referring to.

"My mom's neighbors are all *black hatters*," Mitzi told us.

"Mine aren't black hatters, but they are really superfrum. I'm lost in a sea of *shaytels*," I told them.

"They all seem to wear the same shaytel," Mitzi commented. I knew what she meant. Married ultra-orthodox women have to cover their heads. So, many of them wear wigs called shaytels.

"They all wear long, straight, blondish pageboy wigs, and do you know why?" I asked. My friends looked puzzled, so I answered my own question. "Because under those long, straight-haired shaytels are frizzy, brown curls. If I could pick my own hair, I'd have long straight locks instead of frizz. These women get married, and they get to pick their own hair."

"So they know right away from your hair that you're not one of them," said Caro.

"I've got my own hair, I'm wearing pants, and the real tip off—I get in the car on Saturday," I said.

"They must hate you," said Caro.

Whenever other Jews find out that I live in this shtetl, they assume that I would be hated by my neighbors, and I have to explain that it's not that way. "My family is always getting invited to Shabbos dinner or Shabbos lunch at a neighbor's home. Even strangers invite us.

"Actually, they're very nice. I don't think they care how I handle my Judaism. Some of them are *baal tchuvas*—recently religious—with families that aren't observant. Some come from religious families, some from conservative families or reform and some from families that are totally secular," I told them.

"Once I was at Marshall Field's in the kitchen

department. There was a long wait for the register, and I started talking to this woman next to me. Well, I recognized the pageboy shaytel right away and the neighborhood uniform — long blue jean skirt, and sleeves past the elbows, even in summer. So, I mentioned to her that we must live in the same neighborhood. And, of course, we did. She asked me how I knew that and I explained — the shaytel and long skirt was a give away. Now she knew I was Jewish 'cause I don't think the gentiles in the neighborhood know the word shaytel, so she says to me, 'Can you bring your family to Shabbos lunch tomorrow?'"

"Did you go?" Mitzi asked.

"Yeah, Marv said, 'sure,why not,' and we went. I've gotten friendly with Nehama, the wife, and Marv sometimes works out with Yosef at the J."

"And the great thing is you can't reciprocate. They can't eat in your house because you don't keep kosher," Mitzi explained. "What a deal."

"I do keep kosher-*style*, but even if I kept kosher, it wouldn't be kosher enough because I'm not frum," I added.

"My mom gets invited to the neighbors all the time, and they won't eat in her house, and she does keep kosher," said Mitzi. "She used to get insulted by this — her *kashrut* is suspect because she's not Orthodox, and she eats in regular restaurants — then I told her to enjoy the invitations, and she can send a little gift. And who needs all that work. These families have ten kids. So now Mom seems to enjoy it."

"I couldn't live among them," said Caro.

"It's very nice," I said.

"When I grew up there were no *frum* families," Mitzi explained. "My high school was all Jewish — mostly easy-listening Jews — secular, reform, a few conservative Jews. When they'd pass out a test at Mather High School, it was like reading the Yom Kippur contributions at a reform temple … Bromfman, Dembitz, Goldberg, Goldman, Goldstein, Jacobson, O'Malley."

"There are no Jewish kids at Mather any more. The Jewish kids are all in the religious day schools. I don't know who's left to go to the public schools," I said.

"At least someone's keeping the religion alive," Mitzi said. "Most Jewish kids seem to forget everything by the time the last Bar Mitzvah thank-you card is mailed."

It took me awhile to find my van in the parking lot. We had all agreed we were looking forward to the wedding (although I would have the burden of seeing my husband with a date). While I was searching for my car, I started thinking about all the packing Caro had done, and thought, maybe I should pack up some of Marv's stuff. That way I'd have something to talk about with him if I had to make conversation. I'd just tell him I had a lot of his things ready for him to pick up.

I finally located my van after twenty minutes of searching. When I had pulled in, I parked next to a white pick-up truck. The pick-up truck had left and had been replaced with a silver Jaguar. No wonder I couldn't find my car. I decided I just couldn't rely on other parkers to find my van. I'd have to find another method. I might even have to resort to remembering the numbers posted at each row in the lot.

I wanted to get those big plastic bins, but I was low on gas, so I pulled into a station. After I had set the gas pump in the tank, I got back into my car to wait for the tank to fill. I really wanted those bins, so I thought I'd call the Target near my house to make sure they still had them.

A young man answered the phone. His voice kept cracking, and he sounded just like Richard Crenna's character, Walter Denton, on *Our Miss Brooks,* or maybe, the time he played the young man who had a crush on Lucy in an episode of *I Love Lucy.* I asked him about the bins, and the imitation Walter Denton put me on hold. I kept thinking about Richard Crenna. I couldn't remember if he was still alive. I was anxious to get home to my computer and find out.

The clerk was back. He told me they were sold out of

the bins. I asked him for the number of another Target nearby. I thanked him, and his voice cracked as he said, "You're welcome." I thought he might add, "Miss Brooks."

I called the Target in Niles and was in luck. They still had plenty of bins on sale. I really wanted those bins, so I hung up and started driving out of the gas station. I heard someone frantically yelling in a foreign language. I stopped the car before I got out of the lot and looked back and was dumbstruck.

I had pulled the gas hose out of the gas station pump, and it was dangling from my van. A skinny gas station attendant ran up to me screaming in an unfamiliar language. I put my hand to my forehead and just hung my head for a moment. This was embarrassing, inconvenient, and probably expensive.

The skinny foreigner directed me into the station building and said something to me that sounded like, "Wet for manger," but I assumed he meant I should wait for the manager. He asked me for my license and started writing down information on a report in between checking out patrons' coffee and cigarette purchases. I was forced to wait there feeling like a criminal.

Finally, a big, burly-looking guy with bright orange hair stepped out of the back office and asked me, "You the lady who pulled out the hose?" I told him I was. I was looking pretty embarrassed and shaken up. "Happens all the time. Mostly when folks have been on the phone. I guess they forget about the pump. You want me to contact your insurance agent or do you want to pay me directly?"

"I can give you a check. How much is it?" I asked.

The burly, orange-haired fellow opened the door and yelled at a man who was fixing a hose. "Hey Herb how much is it?" Herb told him it would be eighty-five dollars. "Someone pulled that one out yesterday. Like I said, happens all the time." He took my check and I left, but it felt more like escaping. I was no longer in the mood to drive to Niles to find the bins at Target.

That night laying awake in bed I kept thinking about

the old drive-in theaters. Right after the dancing hot dogs and popcorn sing *Let's Go Out to the Lobby*, they would show a cartoon of a family in their car enjoying the film and the voice-over would say, "Don't forget to put back your speaker."

The father in the car would forget. Then they'd show him driving off, but instead of the speaker getting yanked out of it's stand, the driver's car door would be ripped from its hinges. I was thinking they probably lied. The speaker would come out just like the gas pump, but they couldn't show that. They wanted everyone to worry about their car, so they wouldn't forget to replace the speaker. It was pure propaganda.

I fell into a deep sleep. Suddenly, I was propelled back in time to the old Sunset Drive-In Theater that used to be on McCormick Avenue. I was sitting in the driver's seat of a silver Jaguar watching the screen. I had long, straight, blonde hair. In the back seat were two little boys. The speaker that came in through the window was an old-style headset. The boys in the back kept saying, "Take off your headset, you'll ruin the car."

But I wouldn't listen, and I started to drive off. As I did this, the headset pulled my blonde hair off, and I was left with my short, frizzy, dark hair. The boys in the back started jumping up and down shouting, "We told you so." I turned to them to tell them to be quiet, and I saw they had the faces of Marv and Patrick. When I turned back, I discovered there was now a man in the passenger seat doing a crossword puzzle.

He looked at me and asked, "What's a seven letter word for marriage ceremony?" I recognized him as Richard Crenna's character Luke from *The Real McCoys*.

"Wedding," I answered.

"Good," he said. "We have to pick up Pepino." I pulled the car up to an outdoor skating rink. Someone who looked like Pepino from the old television show was doing twirls and flips on the ice. He started skating towards the car, and suddenly, he and Luke were carrying big, heavy, plastic bins and trying to load them into the car which had changed from a Jaguar to a white pick-up truck.

"What's in those bins?" I asked.

Luke looked at me and said, "Your life." The alarm rang and I woke up.

Chapter Eleven

I *had forgotten to turn off the alarm before I went to bed. It was Saturday; the kids were at Marv's for the weekend. I had intended to catch up on my sleep. I shut off the alarm and tried to go back to sleep, which I can usually do. However, I kept thinking about the book I was writing. Ideas were spinning around in my head. I knew I could not get back to sleep. I went into the kitchen, made a pot of strong coffee, and sat down at my laptop. I had begun leaving it open on my kitchen table. I started writing and had two cups of coffee. I figured I had been writing for about a half an hour. I looked down at my watch to confirm that, but the face was too small to read.*

I had gotten in the habit of typing in fourteen point to avoid needing glasses. I had bought several pairs of reading glasses at Walgreens days earlier and tried keeping them scattered around the house so that there would be a pair in every room. But over the past few days I had failed to put them back in the same place, and they seemed to be lost.

I looked at the clock on my microwave, but it said *stir*.

I looked at the clock on my oven, but it was blinking 12:00. I walked back into my bedroom to look at my alarm clock, and was surprised to discover, I had been writing for over three hours.

Lillian's wedding was that evening, and I had a lot to do. I needed to finish an article about unusual eBay items that had religious significance. There was a Bartlett pear in New Orleans that had rotted in the shape of Paul the Apostle's profile. There was a potato chip that resembled John the Baptist holding someone's head under water, which had been sealed in a lucite box. And there was the Shroud of Hilton, a pillow case from a hotel in Memphis that came back from the laundry with a stain in the shape of Jesus' face.

I wanted to attend a Yoga class. I needed to do my hair, give myself a facial, and with the kids away, finally shave both armpits and both legs. I also had to straighten up around the house because Patrick would be picking me up at my place. This would be the first time he would get a glimpse into my chaotic home.

I made myself some oatmeal and sat down to finish the eBay story, but I kept going back to my book. An hour later, I had finished chapter two of my novel, but the Shroud of Hilton was still a mystery. I hadn't done any research on my article, and I would have to rush out of the house to catch that Yoga class.

I put on my grey cotton Yoga pants and a sweatshirt and was prepared to drive over to the health club, but when I opened the door, I saw that it was a remarkably sunny day. The temperature outside was only about forty degrees, but with the sunshine, it felt warm. This was unusual for late March in Chicago where we often don't experience sunshine until mid July. I figured I would save time if I went for a brisk walk in the neighborhood instead of driving all the way to the club.

I started down my sidewalk towards the sculpture gardens on McCormick Avenue that run along the canal. I passed many of the orthodox Jews walking on their way back from shul or on their way to someone's house for Shabbat lunch. There were large groups of families with eight or nine children each. The people who knew me said, "*Shabbat shalom,*" and I *shabbat-shalomed* them back. The ones who didn't know me said nothing or nodded. They would have no way of knowing I was Jewish since there are very few non-orthodox Jews in the neighborhood. If I were walking around in a skirt, I would be getting shabbat-shalomed by strangers. Whenever Marv and I had a Bar or Bat Mitzvah to attend on Saturday morning, we would come back to the neighborhood, stay in our nice clothes, and take a walk. Strangers would be shabbat-shaloming us right and left, and we thought it was quite charming. It made our part of Chicago feel like a little European village.

I was walking quickly down the path at the gardens and making mental notes on my novel. I noticed a smell of sulfur or rotten eggs and knew immediately how far I'd walked. I looked across the street and I was correct. I was looking at the classic art deco structure that is responsible for getting rid of the city's human waste. I had gone as far as the Water Reclamation District Building. I never called it that. No one does.

It seems every family in the area has a different name for it. My kids and I call it the Stinky Building, but I've heard it called the House at Poo Corner or Smelly Hall. Every adult I knew referred to it by whatever their kids called it. "Linda, can you believe I got a ticket for going four miles over the speed limit and right outside of Flushing Towers?"

The wind was carrying the scent eastward towards the Jewel parking lot. This was usually responsible for the Jewel's temporary rise in the sale of eggs. Subconsciously, shoppers would buy a dozen, even if they didn't need them.

I was about to turn back, when I spotted a mother deer and fawn eating the vegetation that decorates the grounds at the Stinky Building. I wanted to take a closer look. I waited for the traffic light to change. The corner of Howard and McCormick is always busy, so I carefully crossed hoping the deer wouldn't leave by the time I got to the west side of the street. I tiptoed across the grass, getting closer to the pair.

I had never gotten this close to wild deer, and I figured they would run away any minute. The mother kept on eating, but the little one looked at me. Our eyes met and I thought, *now he's going to run,* but he didn't. He started walking towards me. I stood frozen. *Don't come so close,* I was thinking. *You're supposed to be afraid of me not the other way around.* I wanted to run away but thought the deer might chase me.

I took a deep breath and realized that was a crazy notion. Never in my life had I heard of or seen footage of a deer chasing a human. This was Bambi not some dangerous animal. He walked up to me. I put my hand out, and the baby deer rubbed his head on my hand. Then the mother looked at him, she moved her head as if to tell him *we going in this direction,* and they both ran to the far side of the building into a thicket of bushes. It had felt good to touch the fawn. I headed back feeling elated.

I was two blocks from home when someone called my name. I turned and saw Chana Leah Burnstein. We met when my older kids had been in preschool with her youngest kids at the Jewish Community Center. We were always running into each other and occasionally went for coffee. "Shabbat shalom," she said.

"Shabbat shalom."

"How are you?" she asked.

"Fine. How are you and all your kids?" She has eight.

"Wonderful, *Baruch Hashem,*" she answered. "Schmuel and I are going to Jamaica next week, alone." Chana Leah stressed the word *alone.*

"You're kidding?" I said.

"No, Baruch Hashem. He won this trip from his company. Schmuel had the most sales," she explained.

"Mazel tov," I said. "Chana, how do you go to the pool in your long skirt and shaytel?" I asked.

"Oh." She looked around. We were alone. "I'll be wearing a swim suit and my real hair." She looked around again and whispered, "When we're on vacation, we leave the Torah at home." I had heard similar stories from some of my other frum friends. They seemed to confide in me.

Since I'm Jewish, but not Orthodox, I am both an insider and an outsider. "I just hope we don't run into anyone from the neighborhood," Chana Leah said.

"That's unlikely," I added.

"Three years ago Schmuel won the trip to Puerto Rico. There was another couple there from our neighborhood. They were checking in as we arrived at this beautiful resort with three pools. I bought shorts and a one-piece bathing suit for the trip. As soon as the other wife and I saw each other, I knew we were both thinking the same thing—that we can't put on our shorts or take off our shaytels. We both stayed covered up and didn't go to the pools. After five days, I started talking to her, and it was just as I had thought. She admitted she was planning to wear a bathing suit at the pool until they ran into us," she explained.

"Once you both knew about it couldn't you then go to the pool?" I asked.

"If our husbands weren't there, yes. The other men wouldn't be a problem. They're not frum. They wouldn't think anything about seeing our hair or legs. We just couldn't do it with another frum man around. So, we sent our husbands out golfing, and we laid around the pool drinking Mai Tais."

When I got back to my house, I saw that the tulip bulbs in my front yard had begun to sprout. Their yellow and orange flowers were just beginning to show beneath the deep green leaves that were wrapped around the unopened petals. They were like the munchkins in colorful hats who were too shy at first to come out to greet Dorothy. I hoped they would show themselves in the next few days but worried that we might get another frost that would throw them off their schedule. Chicago gardens are at the mercy of Midwest weather. Some years plants bloom in a warm week of March but then die in a May cold spell.

The ground cover was filling in nicely. There were still wood chips in the front garden and a burrito wrapper, which I picked up. For some reason, there is always a wrapper of some kind left by a litterbug in my front yard. There happens to be a little *mom and pop* store located around the block.

I figured that if an inconsiderate person buys a food item, by the time that person gets to the middle of the block, he has finished his food and drops the wrapper right at my house. I looked around for more litter, but there wasn't any. I went into my house to straighten up the rooms.

Four days worth of newspapers were scattered on my couch in the living room. I had planned to read them, but I was getting so far behind and with two Sunday papers about to arrive the next day, I just tossed them in the recycling bin on the porch.

There was a pile of naked Barbie and Ken dolls by the fireplace. When I was a girl, I had one Barbie doll, one Ken doll, and Barbie's friend Midge, who never seemed to catch on. If I wanted a new outfit for Barbie, my mom would get me one. She didn't get me a whole new Barbie. If I wanted Barbie to go to the beach, I got a bathing suit for her.

Now if Delilah wants Barbie to go to the beach, I have to get her Malibu Barbie. It doesn't make sense. When I go to the office, it's still me in office clothes, and when I go to Yoga, it's me in Yoga clothes. I don't need to clone myself and have a second body to dress in breathable cotton drawstring pants, go to the club, and do downward dog.

I gathered up the naked dolls and dumped them in a wicker basket in Delilah's room. They landed in various Kama Sutra positions.

The dining room table was a mess. It was covered with bills, papers, magazines, and the kids' homework. I didn't feel like filing all of it, so I just made neat stacks and placed them on the dining room chairs, then pushed them under the table. This would do as long as Patrick didn't want to sit at the table.

I started running my bath. Pouring some pungent lavender shower gel under the tap, I took a deep breath, closed my eyes, and imagined myself, for a moment, somewhere in the English countryside. I opened my eyes and was immediately transferred back to West Rogers Park on the far north end of the city that had once been the hog butcher to the world. There were no fields of heather within my reach;

there were fields of dirty dishes stacked in my kitchen sink.

I could hear the water running while I went into the kitchen to clean up. The dishes had caked-on food from the day before, and it got me thinking about Lillian. Once when Mitzi was in town, Lillian met us for lunch, and we were talking about all the housework we tend to have, even with once-a-week help. Lillian mentioned that she could never go to sleep if there was a dish in the sink.

Mitzi and I practically blew our Caesar salad croutons out of our noses laughing. We both constantly have dirty dishes in the sink. Ever since that conversation, we would always make fun of Lillian's incredible housekeeping. Both Mitzi and I agreed, we could sleep very comfortably with filthy plates crusting over in the kitchen.

I checked on my bath, which had filled almost to the rim. There was a layer of lavender-scented bubbles on top of the water. I love baths, and everyday I imagine myself taking a long, leisurely, relaxing bath. However, it rarely works out that way. There might be kids banging on the bathroom door, the phone ringing, siblings fighting, an unexpected visitor ringing my doorbell, or even a neighborhood power outage. But this day, I was hopeful. I wanted to relax.

I don't light candles in the bathroom, because I enjoy reading in the tub with a cup of hot tea by my side. I made some Earl Grey and grabbed a book by Barbara Pym, an underrated English writer I enjoy. I like to buy my own paperbacks, because, quite often, I ruin the books with all the humidity in the room. Most of my paperbacks have swelled to unnatural proportions due to this habit.

I had stopped reading borrowed hard covers in the tub, as there have been several book dropping accidents when I had to retrieve the book and quickly place it in my clothes dryer. These incidents were followed up with plenty of dirty looks from Mrs. Anders, the head librarian, at the Northtown branch of the Chicago Public Library.

I started to undress in the bathroom and could view my naked body in the mirror. It was strange because dressed I looked slim, almost thin, but as soon as I took my clothes off,

I looked Rubenesque. All the angles seemed to round out. It must be some trick in the mirror, I thought.

I lowered myself into the hot, lavender-scented bath and was anticipating reading my novel, but as soon as I opened the book, I realized I didn't have a pair of reading glasses. I had to climb out of the tub, wrap a towel around me, and go in search of a pair of readers.

I had a big basket on the dining room radiator which usually housed a pair or two, but on this day, all I could find was an odd assortment of things that had no relationship to each other. There was a half a deck of playing cards, a Barbie shoe, some business cards from people I didn't recognize, a Mah Jong tile (I don't even play), and the cap to a yellow highlighter.

I never seem to throw these things out, because I figure that some day; I might need those business cards; I might find the rest of the deck; I might locate the highlighter that belongs under that cap before it dries out; and perhaps, I'll take up that Chinese/Jewish game.

During my hunt through the house, I did discover my missing stapler, the mate to several of Delilah's socks (which I had already thrown out because I couldn't find the missing mate), and a pair of cherished but misplaced Swarovski crystal earrings. I couldn't explain what motivated me to look in the fridge. However, it did not prove fruitless, as I did find a small pair of reading glasses in the egg bin, a Godiva cherry truffle, and a handful of aging grapes.

With glasses in hand, I went back to the bathroom, this time averting my eyes from the mirror, as I dropped my towel. No use rubbing salt in the wound. There was no way I would have gotten in better shape from those few minutes of searching around the house, plus, I had eaten a piece of chocolate and some overripe grapes. Once again, I immersed myself into the tub. By now the bubbles were beginning to disappear. I began to read my book.

The story involved Caroline Grimstone, the wife of an anthropology professor who is trying to get a paper published in his field. Caroline volunteers to read to an old missionary in a retirement home who happens to have written unpublished papers on the same subject. Soon, Caroline brings her husband to visit the old man, and they manage to steal the papers which her husband uses in his research. Caroline finally feels she has been useful to her spouse.

I was thinking that maybe I should have helped Marv in his practice. Marv mostly saw nursing home patients. Just like the wife in the novel, I could have volunteered in old age homes. I might have gotten friendly with the administrators and gotten Marv more nursing home contracts. Had he been working more, he might not have had time to contemplate whether or not he was happy. We might still be together instead of the two of us anticipating running into each other with dates at a wedding that evening.

The remainder of the day was pleasant and uneventful. I managed to get back to my eBay article. I checked online and saw that the bidding for the Shroud of Hilton had gotten up to fifteen thousand dollars. I took my new red suit out of the closet. It had been so smashed against my other clothes that the jacket was badly wrinkled. I didn't want to risk burning it with an iron, so I hung it in the bathroom and turned on a hot shower. I had to decide which pair of shoes to wear with my suit. My sexy, black, strappy sandals were uncomfortable for walking and dancing, but my comfortable, black pumps were unsexy. I'd be in the same room with Patrick and Marv so I opted for looking good over feeling good. I could always spend most of the evening at my seat turned away from the table with my fashionable feet in full view.

I wanted to make sure I had a fresh pair of pantyhose, so I started digging through my underwear drawer. I couldn't find any and decided to search in Agatha's room. I had given her several pairs of El-AL pantyhose. I found they were the only brand that really lived up to the promise of *one size fits all*. They had also proved to be indestructible and never ran, although they would eventually snag. Agatha had joked that they were great for the weekends because *they never run on Shabbat*. I should have known she'd still have all the hose unopened. Like all her friends, she'd been running around in skirts, barelegged all winter.

I checked on my suit. The wrinkles had come out, but I had left my Pym book on the tub deck and that had doubled in size.

I applied some silicone based product to my hair, and let it wave in all directions. I wanted to start working on my make-up, but as usual, most of it was gone from my bag. My daughters were forever taking my makeup to experiment on each other.

I hunted in both their rooms and came up with some liner, lipstick, blush, and mascara. With those tools in hand, I worked on my face for thirty minutes—just enough time to achieve that *natural look* that was so popular in the magazines.

I needed some accessories and remembered seeing Agatha's earrings all over the floor in her room. I thought she might have some nice dangling ones and hoped I could find two that matched. I was back in her room on all fours crawling under her desk, checking behind her dresser, and peering under her bed. I finally matched up two gold chandelier earrings that would be perfect.

I was ready early and even switched purses, which is something I never do. I'm used to lugging my big, tan, leather Coach bag everywhere. I hate to change purses, because, inevitably, I forget to include an important item when I switch back to my everyday bag and wind up trying to buy groceries with my health club ID instead of my credit card. But this was a special occasion warranting the inconvenience of the switch. I threw a few necessary items into a small black beaded clutch.

Patrick arrived and presented me with half a dozen orange and pink Gerber daisies. Not knowing where any of my vases were, I filled a white porcelain coffee pot with water, placed the flowers in it, and centered the arrangement on my dining room table.

"You look great," he told me, adding, "That's a terrific suit." We were standing in the dining room, and Patrick was looking around. "Is this an historic Chicago bungalow?" he asked. I told him it was. "There's a lot of history in these old houses," he said.

"The basement used to be a speakeasy in the twenties," I told him. "I'd show it to you, but it's a mess right now, and we better be going." We headed over to Lillian's wedding, which was being held at the Purple Hotel (although I still called it the Purple Hyatt).

CHAPTER TWELVE

We took our seats as the harpist played It Had to Be You. *I had wanted to sit in the back, so I could get a good view of everyone – Marv, Jen, Doree, Caro, but an usher directed us to the fifth row. I guessed he wanted to fill the house from the front first. Now I was not in a good position to scout the guests. Everyone arriving from here on in would be seated behind me. I craned my neck around once to see who was coming into the room. There were some familiar faces, probably friends of Lillian's that I had met once or twice years ago. The harpist was picking up the pace with* S'wonderful. *I really wanted to see who was entering the ballroom. I had tucked a small mirror and lipstick into my clutch. I thought about using the mirror, but how long could I apply lipstick? Too bad I couldn't just powder my nose and peer into a compact like a rearview mirror. But this wasn't the 1950s. I never even understood what all that powdering was about. Was there something about the Cold War that caused women's skin to shine?*

While I was contemplating the Eisenhower administration's part in this mid-century dilemma, Caro showed up and scooted between the aisles, parking herself next to me. Before I could introduce her she stuck her hand out to Patrick and said, "Hi, I'm Caro."

As he shook her hand, Patrick announced, "I'm Patrick Rainey."

"The Fourth," Caro added.

"That's right. Nice to meet you," he said.

"My pleasure." Caro was pouring on the charm.

"Is anyone else here?" I asked.

"Mitzi's in the powder room. I picked her up on my way over. Jen and Albert are bringing Doree, and then she has a date meeting her here for dessert and dancing."

"Someone from J-Date?" I asked.

"I guess," she answered.

"Not the fellow who likes baked snacks?" I asked. Caro shrugged *beats me.*

Mitzi joined us. "Patrick," I said. "This is my friend Mitzi Greenberg. Mitzi, this is Patrick Rainey."

"The Fourth," Caro added. She and Mitzi smiled at each other. Patrick grabbed my hand, and I noticed Mitzi and Caro glance at each other once again. We all looked forward as the harpist played *What The World Needs Now.* The lights began to lower, and I could hear the rest of the guests hurriedly taking their seats.

Everyone was facing the front of the room, looking in the direction of the chuppah. It was covered with white roses and baby's breath, and it stood on a riser. The harpist changed from the Bacharach tune to the classic *Here Comes The Bride.*

"This is it," someone said. The harpist began playing a song I dreaded to hear on such occasions, *Sunrise, Sunset.* Barry's parents, a nice-looking older couple, headed down the center aisle towards the platform. Barry's mother was rather tall for a Jewish woman in her seventies. She carried herself well in a cocktail-length, beaded, pale-pink, loose-fitting dress. Her hair was chin-length, straight, blonde, and worn in a blunt cut. She had a surprised look on her face which was either the result of a too tight face-lift or the sign of a thyroid condition.

Barry's father was slightly shorter than his wife. He

wore a well-fitted tuxedo and walked with a slight list to the right. The pair stopped halfway to the chuppah, and while the harpist still played that overused tune from *Fiddler on the Roof*, Barry appeared and was prompted by a broad-shouldered woman to begin his walk down the aisle.

He looked leaner than I remembered and had that gaunt, tight look that I associated with runners. Barry hesitated, so the woman gave him a little nudge, and he began to take small, deliberate steps. Caro leaned towards my ear and whispered, "Dead man walking."

Barry reached the spot where his parents were standing. He kissed them both, then they walked under the chuppah, and stood to one side. Barry waited at the edge of the runner just before the chuppah. The harpist segued into *Thank Heaven For Little Girls*, a tune I felt was too cutesy for the nuptials of a forty-nine-year-old bride.

Lillian's parents, Herb and Evelyn, began their walk. Herb kept stopping to shake hands, and Evelyn kept pulling his arm away so that he'd continue. They stopped halfway down the aisle.

Once again the harpist played *Here Comes The Bride,* and Lillian made her entrance. She was wearing an eggshell, beaded, cocktail-length, flapper-style dress with a matching beaded headband that ran across her forehead — 1920s style. It went well with her short pixie haircut.

Her hair was several shades lighter than its usual dark brown and had reddish highlights. She looked as if she had stepped off the cover of an early twentieth century edition of *Vogue Magazine*. She should've been holding one of those long cigarette holders instead of the nosegay of white roses and baby's breath.

As she approached her parents, I could see that Lillian and her mother shared a sort of ethereal elegance. Lillian reached her parents, they kissed her, and the three of them walked to the end of the aisle where Lillian joined Barry. Her parents went under the chuppah and stood opposite their soon-to-be *machatunim*.

The rabbi seemed to appear out of nowhere and stood

before the couple under the chuppah. I recognized him as Rabbi Teitelbaum from Congregation Beth El Shalom, a new conservative synagogue in Northfield. He looked like a forty-year-old version of Elliot Gould. There had been some controversy surrounding Rabbi Teitelbaum when he was the associate Rabbi at a synagogue in Deerfield (this resulted in the usual goings on—the formation of a new break-away synagogue with half of the old congregants following Rabbi Teitelbaum to the new location). Rabbi T, as I was aware he was often called, welcomed everyone to this auspicious occasion.

Mitzi tapped me on my knee and pointed to the back of the room where Jen, Albert, and Doree were sitting. I smiled at them. Jen rolled her eyes to the left to indicate where Marv and a short-necked, although fairly attractive, woman were seated farther down in the same row. I glanced quickly, then turned forward before they could see me.

Towards the end of the ceremony, Patrick put an arm around me. Rabbi T. placed the traditional glass-rolled-in-a-linen-napkin on the floor for Barry to step on. The riser, on which they all stood, must have been slightly tilted because, as we all prepared to shout *Mazel Tov*, the glass goblet rolled out of the napkin. Barry, who hadn't noticed, stomped down on the napkin, but there was no sound of breaking glass. He must have wondered what went wrong. He stomped down once again on the now flat napkin. Barry wore the expression of a deer-caught-in-the- headlights. Lillian gave him a look as if to say *you idiot — it rolled over there* and pointed to the glass on the floor. Barry, embarrassed, quickly retrieved the goblet, returned to his spot on the riser, and placed the glass back on the napkin, but he forgot to roll it up.

Before Lillian could stop him, he stomped his foot onto it, and shards of glass went flying. Everyone under the chuppah looked horrified, while those in the first two rows screamed and put their hands over their faces.

Patrick leaned close and said, "It's like a Gallagher concert."

"Jack Daniel's — neat, gin and tonic, chablis," said Patrick as he handed a glass to me, Caro, and Mitzi respectively. We were in the adjoining room for the cocktail hour. The receiving line had been cancelled, and we had been herded in, as quickly as possible, for drinks and appetizers. Jen, Albert, and Doree had already had their drinks in hand when we spotted them.

"What do you think is going on in there?" Mitzi asked nodding towards the ballroom where the wedding service had been held.

"Probably setting up a triage unit," said Doree.

"I don't think anyone was hurt that bad," commented Jen.

"There was an awful lot of screaming," said Caro. "And they weren't screaming Mazel Tov."

"I hope no one was hurt," said Mitzi.

"I'm going to find out. I'll ask Shar," said Jen. She handed Albert her drink, which appeared to be something with Diet Coke, and left.

"Who the hell is Shar?" asked Doree.

"She's the wedding planner. Jen knows her. Shar was telling everyone when to walk down the aisle — looks like Mike Ditka in a dress," Albert explained.

The waiters were passing out sushi, vegetable paté on crackers, and mini spanokopeta while the harpist played *What A Day This Has Been*. I caught the buzz of everyone's comments, "Can you believe it ... I've never seen anything like that happen ... poor Lillian."

Jen returned. "Well, they're still cleaning up the blood, mostly superficial wounds."

"Mostly?" Caro asked.

"A few of the guests in the first two rows got hit with flying glass. Luckily, everyone protected their eyes, but some got cuts on their hands. Barry's great-aunt, unfortunately, got a slash on her forehead. The concierge is bandaging them now. The worst was Barry. He got a chunk of glass in his foot. Marvin's working on him."

"How's Lillian?" I asked.

"I haven't seen her. But you can imagine. You know how she likes things perfect."

"Maybe we should act like nothing happened, like we didn't notice," Mitzi suggested.

"Oh brother, how do you not notice blood and gore under the chuppah?" Caro asked. "Hey, that would be a great title for a book—*Blood and Gore Under the Chuppah*," she added.

"Really, just tell Lillian *lovely ceremony*, after all, it was hardly blood and gore," said Mitzi.

"She's right. It's barely noticeable that several guests were injured, and the groom was crippled," said Doree.

"Happens all the time," Caro added.

"In Iraq," said Doree.

"I just hope Marv can save him," said Jen.

"Save him? Barry's injuries aren't that serious?" I said.

"I mean save him from having to go to the hospital. Wouldn't that be awful if he had to go to the emergency room. He could be waiting there for hours and miss the entire reception," said Jen.

A tall, pretty waitress, probably also an actress (Chicago is full of actress/waitresses), approached us with more appetizers. I noticed egg rolls had been added. Albert took one. When the rest of us declined the hors d'oeuvres, the actress/waitress whispered to us, "It'll probably be a while until dinner." We took what was left on her tray and sent Albert and Patrick to get us more drinks.

"He's darling," Doree commented while chewing a spanakopeta.

"Adorable," said Mitzi with her mouth full of paté and cracker.

"He's very nice," was Jen's comment.

"Oh brother Linda, he's hot," said Caro tossing two pieces of sushi into her mouth.

"We're really just friends," I told them choking on an egg roll.

"Yeah!" Doree commented and laughed. I saw the look on her face. She wasn't buying it, nor were my other friends.

The cocktail hour stretched into two. I ran into several of Lillian's friends. One, Helen Dubow, who had also attended the U of I but was a member of the other Jewish sorority house, walked up to us and said hello to Doree.

Doree turned to the rest of us and said, "You remember Helen from STD's."

Jen quickly said, "You mean SDT's." Helen rolled her eyes.

Doree embarrassed said, "That's what I meant."

After Helen walked away, Jen said to Doree, "I can't believe you said STD's instead SDT's."

"Hey, it was an honest mistake."

"But I think she had the clap in college. Don't you remember Lillian telling us?" said Jen.

"Oh, so what?" Caro added.

"Now she'll think Lillian told us," said Jen.

Albert and Patrick were having a discussion about golf. Patrick claimed he didn't have the patience to play the game, while Albert admitted he lived for his weekends on the course.

"Patrick, I tell you, all those hours in the office and the courtroom—I feel claustrophobic all winter. But as soon as the snow melts, I grab my clubs and get out. I just love to go outdoors."

"So we've heard," said Doree.

"What?" asked Albert.

"We've heard you love to *go* outdoors," Doree said looking at each of us.

Albert, scowled, looked at Jen, and said, "You told?"

"Oh brother, Doree, now you got Jen in trouble," Caro whispered.

"He doesn't care. He's putting on an act," said Jen. She was correct, because instantly Albert's scowl turned into a sheepish smile.

"Doesn't care about what?" Patrick asked.

"Never mind," I said.

"You don't want to know," Albert added.

Caro wandered off and disappeared into a whirl of

guests. Lillian and Barry were still not in sight, and neither was Marv. I was glad the actress/waitress had pushed the hor d'ouvres, or we'd all be drunk and starving. The natives were getting restless. Over the strings of *Around The World In Eighty Days,* I could hear murmurings of, "Where are they?… Is he all right? … What's taking so long?" The harpist looked like she needed a break.

I spotted Caro talking to a thin woman with frosted hair. She looked familiar. They seemed to be having quite an animated conversation. The woman was waving her hands in all directions. Caro was nodding.

Caro rejoined our little group. "Who was that?" I asked her.

"Don't you remember Joanne Schwakberg?"

"She used to be a brunette," I said.

"Everyone used to be a brunette," Caro said.

"Is she still married to Billy Brown?" I inquired.

"Yeah, and he's got some huge practice. She was telling me about her new home in Scottsdale. It's got a great view of the mountains."

"Are they moving there?" I asked.

"No. They still live downtown. It's one of her extra homes."

"You mean a second home?" I asked.

"A fourth home. She has two in Florida: Boca and Weston. She says it's an investment, but she spends time at all of them. Billie is constantly working. I heard he's never around. You know the type of surgeon. Arrogant. Can't give his family the time of day. He's not even here with her, and *he's* Marv's friend. So she buys and decorates properties. She's a nice girl. I don't know why she married that jerk. Billy's a terrible husband."

"What she lacks in attention, she makes up for in square footage," Doree piped in.

Jen turned to us and informed us that, according to Shar, the room and the groom were both ready for dinner, and we should head into the ballroom. Patrick and Albert grabbed our glasses and walked over to a standing tray to get rid of them. That's when Shar stopped me.

"Linda, I'm Shar. Thank goodness your husband was here. He really saved the day."

There was no adequate reply for that, so I just said, "He's good with feet."

She went on, "Jen tells me you're dating. I just wanted you to have my card, in case you should need any party planning in the future. Believe me, not all my weddings are this bloody." She handed me her business card. I read her company name, *Till Death Do We Part.*

CHAPTER THIRTEEN

*L**adies** and Gentlemen, please help me welcome, for the first time anywhere, Mr. and Mrs. Barry Ladman," an-nounced Johnnie Kay the bandleader. The Johnnie Kay Quin-tet played* Simon Tov U' Mazel Tov, *as the couple entered the ballroom, Lillian gracefully and Barry, who now sported a surgical shoe on his right foot, lumbered along beside her. Everyone stood, clapped, and joined in singing the joyful Hebrew song of celebra-tion.*

Except for the head table, the room was filled with round tables of ten. Patrick and I were seated with Doree, Mitzi, Jen, Albert, Caro, and three strangers. There was a dark-haired, tall woman about my age named Millie. She introduced herself to us right away and seemed very friendly.

I found I couldn't take my eyes off her face because, although she was not ugly, she had the worst nose I'd ever seen in my life. This wasn't your average big schnoz. The fact is, I find prominent noses appealing. I enjoy Barbara Streisand's profile. I thought Cher was beautiful before her plastic surgery. And, I always liked Susan Lucci who plays Erica Kane on the soap opera *All My Children.*

When I first got hooked on the show, she had her original Roman nose. I thought *here is a real beauty,* but over the decades, her brown hair got lighter, and her nose got smaller. My point is, I'm no small-nose freak. But this was no Bob Hope ski slope. This was Jimmy Durante in a black cocktail dress.

Except for her nose, Millie had great features. If not for a half inch of bulbous flesh, she would be stunning. What impressed me about Millie was her self confidence — that in this day and age of easily attainable cosmetic surgery, she chose to go through life looking like a probiscus monkey.

Also at our table were a father and son pair. The son, Norman, was fortyish and nerdy. The father, Walt, was incredibly good-looking for an older man. He possessed a full head of thick, white hair. He seemed to be well built and wore a dark-blue cashmere jacket with an expensive-looking tie. Walt explained that he was semi-retired from his nanotechnology company and was looking forward to Norman taking over the reigns full-time.

I wasn't quite sure what nanotechnology was, but I knew it had something to do with small things and appreciated the irony that he was seated next to Millie's large nose.

Norman, who was married, had left his wife home in St. Louis. Walt, who had also traveled from St. Louis, was divorced. When he had explained this, I could see Mitzi, who was sitting to the left of Doree, elbow her. At the same time, I could tell that Caro, who was seated on the other side of Doree between her and Millie, was elbowing Mitzi on her right side. I even sensed that Mitzi was elbowing Millie with her other arm. Mitzi looked like she was about to do the *Chicken Dance.*

Marv must have been seated on the other side of the dance floor, because I still couldn't see him. Barry's father made the *Ha Motzi* over the challah and pre-cut squares were dispersed to every table. Patrick commented that it was great challah.

Caro told Patrick she didn't believe he was Jewish, even though I was sure I had told her that he was. To prove his Hebraic roots, Patrick boasted that not only would he sing *Adon Olam*, but that he could do it to any tune. Mitzi suggested he sing it to the tune of *Oh Danny Boy*. Patrick knew all the words and the prayer fit the Irish ballad perfectly. Caro suggested *Memories* from Cats. Patrick replied with perfect pitch. Doree asked for *Makin' Whoopee*, and I thought if Millie came up with *Inka Dinka Doo*, I might lose it.

Our little game was interrupted by the tinkling of many glasses. Barry stood up and started to thank his wife Lillian for all she had done and for putting up with him. I thought that was something you did for anniversaries — thanked your spouse for putting up with you all these 15, 25, 30, or whatever years. Lillian had only put up with Barry for a few hours, granted, they were drama-filled hours.

Barry asked Marv, who was seated across the room, to stand. He thanked Marv for having the good sense to always carry his bag and supplies in his car. This made Marv sound like a drug dealer. Marv did always carry these things with him, because he went from one nursing home to another throughout the course of his working day.

Marv looked good and not at all embarrassed, which I thought strange since he never enjoyed being in the spotlight. I could hear Millie ask Caro who Marv was and Caro replying, "Linda's husband." There was a pause in their exchange, and then Millie asked, "Then who's Patrick?"

"Linda's date," Caro said.

"Wow," Millie whispered. She was as impressed with my love life as I was with her profile.

Johnny Kay had the married couple get up and dance, although it turned out to be more like rhythmic hobbling. Then the bandleader encouraged everyone else to join in. The quintet was playing *Smoke Gets In Your Eyes*. It should've been *Glass Shards Gets In Your Eyes*.

Patrick led me to the dance floor. He was a fairly good dancer, not as good as Marv. Marv and I had studied ballroom dancing before we had kids and had always danced well together, our small height disparity being a contributing factor. Patrick, being so much taller than me, made me feel insignificant in his arms. He moved well, but my face was stuck in his chest. He smelled great—a mix of cinnamon and wood chips.

A photographer was negotiating the dance floor turning right and left, every few seconds. He would stand still, adjust his lens, snap the picture, then pivot like a dancer to take someone's candid photo behind him. He was wiry and had longish salt and pepper hair.

He pointed his camera at us, so Patrick and I stopped dancing for a second to pose. We smiled. The photographer adjusted his lens, but before he could take our picture, he spun on his heels and snapped Lillian's parents. I said to Patrick, "Maybe he used to photograph runway models."

"Maybe he used to be a runway model," Patrick said.

I expected to find Marv and his date on the dance floor, but I didn't see them. Patrick and I went to sit down. The music changed to *For All We Know*. I felt a tap on my right shoulder. It was Marv. He looked at Patrick and said, "You don't mind," then whisked me onto the dance floor.

Did I imagine hearing Patrick say, "But I do mind."? Before I knew it, I was foxtrotting with Marv in perfect synchronization like the old days. Without speaking, he led me around the dance floor, weaving gracefully between the other dancers. The photographer pivoted, pirouetted, and pranced between the dancing couples, shooting away madly. Out of the corner of my right eye, I noticed Millie dancing with Walt.

"We should have kept up our dancing," Marv said, as if that would have helped.

"You seemed to have kept yours up." I was sorry the instant I said that. I didn't mean for it to be a double entendre. Hoping he hadn't noticed, I quickly added, "Why aren't you dancing with your girlfriend?"

"Katie's not my girlfriend."

"Your date then."

"Well, she doesn't dance."

"Too bad," I said.

"Not really. I was hoping to dance with you."

"Won't Katie mind?"

"Not at all. She's in favor of it," Marv answered.

"That's very open-minded of her," I said.

"You look wonderful," Marv said, then added, "but you always do." I guess he had forgotten the mornings I awoke with my kinky hair all smashed together on my crown and him telling me, "You look like Zippy the Pinhead."

Marv dipped me at the song's conclusion, and I headed back to my table. Like a tornado, someone twirled in my path and stopped in front of me. It was that pivoting photographer. I noticed he had a nice face — good features — a wide grin with white teeth.

"Are you Linda Grey?" he asked

"Yes." He pivoted and got a quick shot a couple walking past us.

"I did your wedding," he told me. He adjusted his lens, knelt down, and got a long shot of someone across the room.

"You did?" I would have remembered him.

"I was working with Gary Pozner, Pozner Photography." I remembered that name. *Pivot, Click ...* Another photo taken. "Back then I was Gary's assistant. Hadn't developed my own style yet." Three hundred and sixty degree pirouette, *click,* and a close-up of me. He certainly had his own style now. "Philip Pfeffer Photography," he announced as he reached inside his sport coat and handed me his card. I thanked him as he turned and whirled away

"I almost forgot how well you two dance together," Caro whispered to me.

I was back at the table picking at a raspberry and goat cheese salad. Patrick and Albert were talking sports. Doree, Jen, and Mitzi were playing Jewish geography with Norman. I soon discovered Mitzi's husband has an aunt in Creve Couer, Jen's neighbors were originally from St. Louis Park, and Doree knew some tennis pros from Ladeau.

Walt and Millie appeared to be having an intimate discussion, but I couldn't make it out. Patrick turned to me, placed his arm around my shoulder, and said, "I was getting jealous watching the two of you dance."

"We took classes years ago. But you're very coordinated. You could dance like that with a few lessons," I said.

"I'm not jealous of how well Marv dances, only that he was dancing with you." I wasn't quite sure how to react to that, but before I could reply, Johnnie Kay was back at the microphone introducing a vocalist, Esmerelda-Lee.

She was wearing a tight-fitting, slinky gown made of red and silver paillettes. Her hair was piled on top of her head with loose curls cascading down. She looked very familiar. Esmerelda-Lee took the microphone and started singing Gershwin's *Love Walked In*.

Walt and Millie sauntered over to the dance floor. Patrick grabbed me and led me to the dance floor. I could see Jen get up and pull Albert up to dance, but he pulled her back down, so she sat there grudgingly.

Patrick held me close. I took a deep breath of the cinnamon and wood chip scent, which now had a note of goat cheese to it. Patrick was humming along with Esmerelda-Lee. As she sang the words, "One look and I had found my future at last," I thought he kissed the top of my head, which made me feel self-concious because I knew I had applied a lot of product. He went back to humming.

Esmeralda-Lee sang, "One look and I had found a world completely new when love walked in with you," and then I felt something that was definitely a kiss on the neck. It felt good. I preferred he kiss my neck (where I had only applied a dab of lavender oil) instead of my head (where I had schmeered gobs of Frizz-Eaze Firm-Holding Gel).

"Hi there." That was Marv's voice. He and Doree were dancing alongside of us. I could tell Patrick was trying to dance us away from them, but Marv was too smooth a dancer. Even with Doree on his arm, he could effortlessly follow us. The song ended, and I told Patrick, "Let's sit." Doree followed us back to the table. "What was that about?" I asked her under my breath.

"Marv came over to say hi. Caro told him about my

date coming later for dessert and dancing, and he thought I could use a refresher course. Well, I haven't danced in ages."

"Well, don't dance near us. I may be crazy, but I think Patrick wants to be alone with me," I explained.

"Linda, doesn't the singer look familiar?" asked Mitzi.

"I thought the same thing," said Jen.

"She does," I added.

"She must have gone to school with us," said Caro. A tall actor/waiter was going around the table giving everyone their choice of red or white wine. I chose white. Patrick chose red.

"I think I'd remember someone named Esmeralda-Lee," said Jen.

"That can't be her real name," said Caro.

"I guess you haven't figured it out yet, but she plays the harp," said Norman.

"How would we know that?" asked Doree.

"Norman's right," said Patrick. "She's the harpist."

They were right. Esmeralda-Lee had changed her hair from a low ponytail to the up-do and changed out of her white blouse and black pants to her evening garb. She must have applied more makeup and false eyelashes.

Esmeralda-Lee started singing *Some Enchanted Evening*. "Let's dance," said Patrick. I could see Jen trying to pull Albert off his chair, but he remained rooted. Again I was in Patrick's arms. I inhaled deeply and got a big whiff of cinnamon, wood chips, goat cheese, and merlot.

"Hi again." It was Marv dancing with Caro.

"What are you doing?" I said to Caro.

"Poor kid has no one to dance with," Marv answered for her. Patrick danced us away from them.

"Esmeralda-Lee was singing from Rogers and Hammerstein's South Pacific, "Once you have found him, never let him go." Philip Pfeffer got between Marv and Patrick and me and began pivoting and clicking. The song ended; everyone returned to their seats.

The main course was served, salmon encroute with garlic potatoes and baby asparagus. Some more speeches were made. Everyone from Barry's family welcomed Lillian into the fold. Everyone from Lillian's family was glad to add Barry to their brood.

Lillian's mother asked Marv to stand, thanked him for his quick thinking and strong podiatric skills, signaled Johnny Kay, who turned to his musicians, and they struck up *For He's A Jolly Good Fellow.* Marv looked unusually comfortable. His date was smiling, which surprised me. I thought she might be angry that he danced so often with other women.

"Marv must feel great. He's the hero of the evening," Caro said.

"Imagine how I feel, I'm dating the hero's wife," Patrick said boastfully with a smile on his face.

So, we were officially dating. We weren't just friends attending an event together. Patrick wasn't just Katherine's good-looking stepson helping me out because he liked my writing. Instead of being some jilted wife approaching fifty, I was a forty-something, not-quite-single woman in a budding relationship with a sexy, younger man. That put quite a different spin on it. I sat up a little taller.

"I notice you have very good posture," said Millie.

"Thank you Millie. I've been practicing Yoga," I told her.

"I enjoy that also. I love the deep breathing," she said and then, as if to demonstrate, she exaggeratedly inhaled through her nose. I was afraid she might suck up one of her baby asparagus through a nostril. I quickly looked away, but my eyes caught Doree's eyes. By the way her pupils dilated, I knew she was thinking the same thing. I choked on a piece of garlic potato.

"Doree, when is your date going to be here?" Caro asked. Doree looked at her watch and told us it would be soon. Jen suggested we take Doree to the ladies room and give her a quick make-over. She had showed up wearing only lipstick and even that was long gone. Caro, Doree, Mitzi, Jen, and I headed to the ladies room.

Chapter Fourteen

*W*e *gathered around Doree who was now sitting in the lounge area of the powder room. We all took out whatever makeup we had with us. All I had tucked into my clutch was lipstick, but Jen and Caro always carry a full bag of supplies. They each wanted to do Doree's face, so it was finally decided that Jen would do her eyes and Caro would do lips and blush.*

"Marv really saved the day," said Mitzi.

"Yes he did," I said. I didn't want to say too much; I could hear someone in one of the toilet stalls.

"I wish Allen could dance like that," said Mitzi.

"I wish Albert would dance," said Jen. "I can't get him up on his feet for anything but golf."

"Marv is really putting on the charm tonight," said Caro.

"It's like he got a dose of Cary Grant," said Doree while Jen was applying mascara. A toilet flushed. An older woman came into the lounge, washed her hands, arranged her hair in the mirror, and left. We were alone now.

"That Millie's a nice lady," said Jen.

"She really is," said Mitzi. There was a moment's silence as if we were each waiting for the other to say the obvious.

"Did you know she has a Ph.D. in chemistry?" asked Jen.

"And she's working on a fat-free oil for frying." Mitzi told us as I wondered if all Millie's projects were so alliterative. We were all silent once again.

"She's very unusual," Doree said, finally breaking the silence.

"Oh brother, is she ever," Caro burst out.

"I know," said Doree. "It's like a shoe in the middle of her face."

"Be quiet," Jen whispered. "Anyone can walk in here. I give her credit. She must have a great deal of self-confidence."

"And Walt seems to be interested," said Mitzi.

"She's already been married twice, she told me," said Caro. I thought it was wonderful that Millie didn't let her nose get in her way.

"I just keep thinking of that *I Love Lucy* episode," said Caro. "The one with William Holden where Lucy keeps bothering him at the Brown Derby, then Ricky brings William Holden back to their hotel to meet Lucy. She doesn't want him to recognize her as the lady from the restaurant."

"I remember," I said. "Lucy makes a fake putty nose."

"It might have been chewing gum," said Caro.

"That's right. Anyway, she's introduced to William Holden, and she has this big fake nose. She's drinking coffee, and the heat from the coffee starts to melt her nose. It just keeps getting longer and hangs over her mouth," I said.

"It's hysterical," said Caro.

"And Ricky's making that face when he can't believe what Lucy's up to. You know, his eyes are bugged out, and he's speechless," I said demonstrating.

"And Lucy's acting like nothing's wrong until she lights up a cigarette, her nose catches fire, and she has to put it out in her coffee," Caro explained.

"That was a great show," said Mitzi.

"But why wouldn't she have it fixed? That's what I don't understand," said Caro.

"Everyone's not as superficial as you," said Doree.

"So, you would walk around with that on your face?" Caro asked.

"Hell no," was Doree's answer.

"That's what I mean. Why wouldn't she fix it?"

"Maybe she's afraid of surgery," Jen offered.

"That could be it," Caro said.

"Or, she can't afford it. I don't think research pays that well," said Mitzi.

"Maybe she just doesn't see it," Mitzi said.

"That can't be it. Doesn't she have to look into microscopes and things like that?" said Caro.

"Maybe she comes from a culture that appreciates large noses," Mitzi said.

"She's a Jew from Buffalo Grove," Doree explained.

"I gotta find out. It just doesn't make sense," said Caro.

"You be nice. She's a sweet girl," warned Jen.

"Hey, I'm always nice," said Caro. I noticed Doree roll her eyes.

"I saw that," said Caro.

"Just doing my vision exercises," said Doree. Another older woman walked in and went into a toilet stall.

"Ok, we discussed you-know-who's you-know-what, so now you all know the rule," said Jen. We all knew what she was referring to. When we were rushing prospective members of our sorority house, we would have a meeting and discuss each girl. We had a rule that we had to end each discussion on a good note about the person. We couldn't go on to the next candidate until we did this, and so inevitably, we would end it on *she has nice hair*. The woman came out of the stall and washed her hands.

"All right, all right ... somebody," said Caro. The woman started to walk out.

Doree raised her hand and said, "She has nice hair."

The older woman turned to us, smiled, and said, "Thank you dear."

Caro finished applying blush to Doree's cheeks. "That looks good," Caro said as she put her makeup back in her purse. A woman in a long, green, satin skirt and sleeveless blouse showing off her buff arms entered the lounge and went into one of the toilet stalls. I walked up to Doree and unbuttoned the top two buttons of her blazer.

"Hey!" said Doree.

"You looked like a nun," I said over the flushing sound in the stall.

"Linda's right," said Jen pulling Doree's collar further apart. "That looks good. You're already for your date."

The woman in the green skirt came back into the lounge and began washing her hands. She looked at us in the mirror. "Aren't you Lillian's friends from AEPhi?" she asked.

We told her we were. She explained she was Lillians's girlfriend from high school, Ava Bernstein. We all remembered her, but we hadn't seen Ava in years. She wiped her hands dry with the ecru-colored paper hand towels embossed with the names Lillian and Barry.

"Nice seeing all of you. I'll see you in there. They're putting out the dessert buffet now," Ava said. She left.

"Ava's got great arms," said Mitzi. "Do you think she works with a trainer?"

"Mitz, when a forty-nine-year-old Jewish woman shows up at an event in March wearing a sleeveless blouse, you can make book on the fact that she's been working with a trainer," Caro said as we all nodded in agreement.

Millie came into the ladies room. She went up to the vanity and started digging in her purse. "I just had to sneak in here. I know it's a bad habit, and I shouldn't be doing this but ..." Millie started to pull a case out of her purse. I thought she was going to light up a cigarette, which I worried would trigger insane laughter from my friends after our Lucy conversation. Instead, she pulled out her cell phone and turned to us. "It's a bad habit—constantly checking my messages."

She was dialing while speaking. She put the phone to her ear, listened awhile, then said, "Nothing." She put her phone away. We were all touching up our makeup.

"Bad news?" I asked while futzing with my hair.

"No news. I'm waiting for the results of an important test at my lab," Millie told us. I saw Caro's eyes light up.

"Millie," Caro said. "I was just wondering why you chose chemistry over some other field of science ... like ... oh, I don't know ... medicine, for instance. Or, maybe you don't like all that blood and cutting."

"Actually, I considered medicine. I have a masters in biology. I even watched my own knee replacement surgery, which I found fascinating. But, I didn't want to go into practice. I prefer research."

"That's great you enjoy your work, but I hear researchers are grossly underpaid," said Caro.

"Caro, really," said Jen.

"I don't mind. I always ask questions myself. Believe me, I've been called nosy more than once." When Millie said that, I purposely avoided eye contact with my friends. "And it's true, about research paying very little." Caro smiled knowingly at us.

"Usually, that's true," Millie went on, "however, fortunately, my field is the exception. You would not believe the amount of huge grants available for the research in my area of expertise. All these big conglomerates have holdings in food companies. And each one wants to be the first one with the next breakthrough in kitchen science. It's extremely lucrative."

"How's your eyesight?" Mitzi asked, joining in on the interrogation.

"What?" asked Millie.

"What she means is, we all wear contacts or glasses, except Linda—who needs to. You're not wearing glasses so Mitzi probably wondered if you're wearing contacts," said Jen.

"I'm happy to say I have twenty-twenty vision," Millie told us.

"Where did you say you were from?" Doree asked her. "Lovely Buffalo Grove," Millie answered. I could tell Caro was really puzzled. Millie wasn't afraid of surgery, she had the finances, good vision, and she was from *lovely Buffalo Grove*. So that was her secret. She was an optimist. She just saw the best in everything.

"Doree, I think your date might be here," she said, then turning to the rest of us, "The dessert buffet is up."

"The Jewish dessert buffet—that sociological phenomenon otherwise known as the running of the bulls," Mitzi said on her way out.

"Maybe they'll have chocolate-covered pretzels for your date," Caro said to Doree.

"He's not the baked-goods dude," Doree said as she followed them out of the ladies room.

CHAPTER FIFTEEN

Back at the party, a crowd had gathered around the dessert *buffet. I spotted Patrick somewhere in that sea of sweet-seeking revelers and was surprised to see who was talking to him. It was Habib from the Cafe Kotel. I joined them. "It's wonderful to see you. Are you catering the desserts?" I asked Habib as Doree approached us.*

Habib kissed Doree, she turned to me and said, "He's catering to me." Well, well, he certainly wasn't the baked-goods-ophile.

"Anyone want some?" Caro asked us as she held out a plate of taiglach, petit fours, and chocolate-covered halavah.

"How did you get past that sea-of-dessert-searching humanity?" Patrick asked her.

"I went around the back. There was a twenty second break when Lillian's Aunt Hilda moved her walker and Uncle Hershel adjusted his toupee. I slipped in surreptitiously."

"Good work Agent X. We'll send you on the next reconnaissance," said Habib.

"Agent X, meet Agent Y," Doree said as Habib and Caro shook hands. Caro was still holding the plate of sweets when unknown arms reached in between us to get at the dessert samples. In an instant the sweets were gone. I really wanted to try some of that halavah.

"I'll get some more," I offered.

"No, you stay with your friends. I'll get some," Patrick said.

"That's okay. I need the exercise. Dodging in between Lillian's relatives will be a good workout," and with that, I disappeared into the crowd of craving guests. The buffet table was about twenty-feet long. There was a kitschy chocolate fountain in the center for dipping fresh fruit and little squares of pound cake. On either side of the fountain were identical dessert set-ups: petit fours, gooey taiglach, two different kinds of halavah (marble chocolate-covered and vanilla chocolate-covered), a two foot croquenbusch, mandel bread, rugalach, mun cookies, sephardic corabiens, pecan pie, chocolate-layered cakes, fruit torts, profiteroles, eclairs, napoleons, various flavored cheesecakes, and a make-your-own-sundae station. I loaded up two plates and barely got out of there alive.

I felt someone pinch my ass, but when I turned, everyone was loading their plates, except for Uncle Hershel, who was adjusting his toupee. A tall, very blond, fortyish gentleman with a British accent asked me if that was the bar that was so crowded.

"No, it's the dessert table," I explained.

"Where's the bloody bar?" he asked. I pointed to the bar across the room. It was manned by a bored-looking bartender who hadn't had many customers all evening. I saw his eyes light up as the Englishman approached him.

Caro walked up to me. "Have you ever been to a wedding with a cash-bar?" she asked me.

"Not a Jewish wedding, but I did go to one in LaPorte," I told her.

"Jewish weddings are always open-bar, but really, they hardly ever unload any liquor," she told me. I remembered all the wine and whiskey Marv and I had lugged back home after our wedding.

"What they should really do at Jewish weddings is keep the open-bar but have a cash dessert buffet." I agreed with Caro that the host would certainly clean up in such a scenario. "Uh oh, Uncle Hershel," she said as she disappeared into a crowd of people.

I joined Patrick, Doree, and Habib back at the table where our actor/waiter was pouring coffee. The quintet started playing *The First Time Ever I Saw Your Face,* and the four of us got up to dance. I leaned my head against Patrick's chest and smelled cinnamon, wood chips, goat cheese, merlot and halavah.

"Doree dances well with her date," I heard Marv say as he and Mitzi danced alongside of us. She gave me a sheepish grin.

"Mitzi!" I said.

"I want to dance too," she said.

"It's tax season. I have to step into Allen's dancing shoes," Marv explained.

"Your husband sure gets around. I haven't even seen him dance with his own date," Patrick commented.

"That's not like him," I said.

"You've observed him on many dates?" he asked.

"No, but he wouldn't leave his date alone ... I don't get it," I said.

"Well, she doesn't seem to mind. Look." Patrick was right. Marv's date was at their table talking and laughing with others. She didn't appear concerned about her date's behavior at all. Esmeralda-Lee finished her Roberta Flack impression, and we sat down.

Jen and Albert returned to the table carrying dessert plates. Jen had some fruit from the chocolate fountain. Albert had managed to grab the top six inches of the croquenbush, point and all. "I can't believe you're going to eat that whole thing," Jen said.

"It's okay, I'll get rid of it on the golf course next week," Albert assured her.

"I'll bet," said Doree as she and Habib sat down.

"Albert means he'll work it off on the course. He's going to Phoenix Wednesday," Jen explained.

"Either way," said Albert as he shrugged his shoulders and smiled.

"You could burn it off by dancing with me," Jen suggested.

"You know I don't dance," Albert said.

"Oh, come on," Jen urged. The band was playing *Autumn Leaves*.

"Maybe when they play a fast song I like," Albert said.

"When you say *maybe* do you mean *possibly* or do you mean *no*?" Jen asked.

"No," Albert answered.

The song ended and Esmeralda-Lee went right into *When A Man Loves A Woman*. This time it was I who grabbed Patrick and led him to the dance floor. We had danced so much this evening that I no longer noticed the height discrepancy.

"I love this song." That was Marv's voice. He was dancing next to me with Jen. I gave her a what-are-you-doing look.

"Well, Albert won't dance," she said as Patrick danced us in another direction. When we returned to our table, Philip Pfeffer was waiting. He wanted to take our table photo. Pivoting around as he arranged us, he finally got us in the position he wanted. Patrick and I were standing behind Millie and Walt. Philip started walking away from the table but kept pivoting to look back at us to make sure we stayed where he wanted.

When he got about fifteen feet from the table, he turned, looked at us, adjusted his lens, and said, "Hold it." Then he began a slow step, step, pivot, step, step, pivot, during which I heard Walt comment, "Isn't that the opening number from *A Chorus Line*?" Philip stopped, took our photo, and immediately pivoted over to the next table. I was still standing when Johnny Kay's musicians struck up a very loud *Hava Nagilla*.

People started rushing to the center of the room. I felt

someone grab my right hand and pull me into the crowd. Someone grabbed my left hand, and I was part of the hora circle. I could see Caro across from me. She was between a teenage boy and Uncle Hershel. I realized I was between Marv and his date. But Marv was on my left side. So, it was his date who had pulled me into the circle.

Marv's date turned to me. Becuase the band was really loud, it sounded like she said, "Hyram Gatie."

"What?" I asked puzzled.

Again, I heard, "Hyram Gatie." Then I remembered her name was Katie and realized she was saying, "Hi, I'm Katie."

I couldn't understand why Marv's date would be so friendly, but I figured *when in Rome,* so I said, "Hi, I'm Linda." As I was being pulled along the hora circle, I noticed most of the dancers were not in sync. Some guests were doing a step, step, step, kick combination, while others were doing a step, step, kick combination, and still some were just doing kick, kick, kick.

The circle was getting bigger and bigger. It finally split into two dance circles, one within the other. The outside circle was moving clockwise with the inner circle going counter-clockwise. Most of the guests had joined the circle. I could see my table was empty and wondered if Jen finally got Albert to get up and dance. I saw Jen in the inner circle between Norman and Walt. I looked for Albert, but the circles were moving too fast. Then I saw that he was at the bar with the Englishman clinking brandy snifters.

Two elderly women got into the center of the smaller circle and started do-si-doing. They would link elbows, dance around and then link the opposite elbows, and do it again in the other direction. Then four older gentlemen surrounded them and started doing the *kazatzkes.* Three of the men couldn't get down very low but one older man was really quite good kicking his legs out from under him and squatting close to the ground.

Now both circles had stopped moving and everyone was standing in place clapping and observing the action in the center. Katie nudged me and yelled, "You're a wonderful dancer."

"Thank you," I yelled back.

"You and Marv dance great together," she said.

I wasn't used to getting compliments from my husband's dates, so I just shrugged and said, "Well." I turned towards the center to see that both Barry and Lillian were in the air on chairs being hoisted by eight male guests—one holding each chair leg. Barry seemed comfortable with this, but Lillian wore a frightened expression on her face. The lifters kept hoisting her up and down. The look on her face turned to panic. Barry saw Lillian's face, he yelled for the lifters to stop, but they couldn't hear him over the raucous revelry. Barry reached out to grab Lillian's hand. Just as he was reaching for her, the four men carrying Lillian's chair moved away from the group carrying Barry's chair, and he fell off of his seat landing on his foot, the one with the surgical shoe.

"Is this a typical Jewish wedding?" asked the Englishman.

"Not really, there's usually more injuries," Albert answered.

I had joined them at the bar for a scotch—neat. We were waiting to find out how Barry was doing. He had been carried out by two guests with Marv at his side.

"I'll have what she's having." That was Caro letting the bartender know she wanted a drink. He seemed appreciative.

"Barry's not the only one who was injured in that hora. My tuchas is sore. I got pinched by Uncle Hershel and the captain of the Evanston High School junior debate team," Caro told me.

The band was playing *You Always Hurt The One You Love*. Shar was milling about the room—I assumed, to inform all the guests regarding Barry's condition. She came over to the bar.

"How's Barry?" I asked her.

"Marv says Barry's going to be fine. I think he's just a little shaken."

"You know, if Barry survives the wedding, I think the marriage stands a good chance," the Englishman said.

Lillian and Barry started walking back into the ballroom holding hands. In addition to the surgical shoe, Barry now sported an ankle brace. Philip Pfeffer escorted them over to a big group of Lillian's relatives. He wanted to take the bride's-side-of-the-family photo. Barry and Lillian took their places in the two chairs in front of the relatives.

Lillian stood up, "Wait a second," she said. "Where's Aunt Hilda?" Everyone started looking around the room.

"She's over here," a bald man shouted from one of the dinner tables. Barry and Lillian started yelling for Aunt Hilda to join them, but she refused. The bald man shouted, "She says if you wanted her in your family picture, you wouldn't have seated her so far from the head table." Barry gave Lillian a look like *it's your side of the family.*

"What a *kvetch*," Caro said to me.

"What's a Jewish wedding without kvetching?" I asked.

"A gentile wedding," Caro answered.

I saw Lillian's mother and another woman about the same age walk swiftly over to Aunt Hilda, place her walker in front of her, and then link arms with her.

They escorted her over to the group. They placed her among the relatives. She was trying to leave, but they smiled and held her still while Philip pivoted and shot the photo. He was too fast for Aunt Hilda. She immediately returned to her table. She was pretty quick for a woman with a walker.

Johnny Kay was playing *All Shook Up*. Out of nowhere, Marv grabbed me. Before I knew it we were jitterbugging like old times.

"Remember the combination?" he asked.

"I don't know," I answered.

"Well, you better, 'cause here we go." And with that, he started the routine we used to do: a cuddle, a pretzel, some more dance steps ending in swinging me over his right hip, his left hip, then sliding me under his spread legs, and bringing me back to standing position. It worked perfectly. Marv could still lift me, of course, I didn't weigh any more than I had the last time we'd danced like that years ago. The song ended. It seemed as if everyone was watching and applauding. I saw that Patrick was standing near the dance floor and had been among those watching. Norman was whispering something to him.

"What was Norman saying to you?" I asked Patrick when I get back to his side.

"He said what everyone's been saying, 'Your date and her husband dance great together.'"

"Ooh, sorry," I said.

"Don't be. It's true."

"I've had enough dancing for one night," I said.

"You sure?" Patrick asked.

"Absolutely."

"I'll get our coats." He headed towards the coat check. I went off in search of Lillian to say goodbye.

Shar stopped me. "I hope you had a wonderful evening," she said.

"Very memorable," I replied.

"You have my card if things work out. And, if things go in the other direction, I do some really lovely *Renewing Our Vows* parties. After congratulating Lillian, I went in search of Patrick. Katie stopped me.

"It was nice meeting you. Marv just went to get his medical bag from the manager's office. I wanted you to know he's been doing a lot of work these past months. He's really quite a guy. I thought you should know."

CHAPTER SIXTEEN

*L*ooking *back on it, I can see that inviting Patrick in after the wedding might not have been such a wise choice. Then again, I would've had no way of knowing what would happen, and how it might effect someone else. I didn't sleep that night and was exhausted Sunday. I worried all day until the kids got home Sunday evening.*

I was putting dishes in the dishwasher when Marv dropped the kids off in front of the house, as usual. Delilah ran up to me and gave me a hug. "I missed you, but Agatha and I watched movies and played *Guess Who* last night," she told me.

"That's great honey," I said.

"Yeah, it was fun," Agatha said then turned to her sister and said, "Loser," and ran towards her room with Delilah trailing after her. I tried to give Drake a hug, but he just walked past me, went into his room, and closed the door. I followed him and knocked.

"Can we talk?" I asked.

He didn't open the door but said, "I'm not mad." I figured that was good. Then he added, "I'm just disappointed." I always thought those were words that kids dreaded to hear, and now I knew why.

"Drake, just let me explain." He opened the door and took me into the kitchen.

"Sit down and talk softly. I don't want the girls to get upset," he said in a quiet voice. I couldn't believe how mature he was acting—and worrying about his sisters' feelings. This was a new development. "When I walked in last night at one-in-the-morning, I might add, I got a little surprise."

"Why didn't you let him explain? He said you just ran out," I said.

"Dad let me take his car last night. I had forgotten my cell phone and stopped home late at night to get it. Imagine my shock when I saw a strange man sitting on our couch wearing a bathrobe, not just any robe, Dad's bathrobe."

"There is an explanation," I told him.

"Unless you've started a new charity called Lounge Wear for the Homeless, I can't imagine what it is."

"That was my date Patrick. I did invite him in last night but only for some hot chocolate ..."

"Is that the term they're using now?" he interrupted me.

"Really. I made him hot chocolate, and I was going to have tea. I gave him his cup, and he went over to the dining room table to sit. I went into the kitchen to get my tea. Patrick pulled out a chair and sat down, but I had stacked all the papers from the table onto the chairs earlier in the day, so when he sat they slid off causing him to slip and spill his chocolate." I could tell Drake knew I was telling the truth.

"You remember I did that piece about getting out stains?" I asked.

"Mom, I rarely read your stuff."

"But you do remember I was trying out different methods on your clothes."

"Yes, you saved my Lakers' jersey."

"So, I knew I had to apply club soda as soon as possible

to the stain and blot it then put it in the dryer. I gave Patrick a robe. He changed in the bathroom. I was downstairs putting his pants in the dryer when you walked in and assumed the worse." Now he knew the truth, but he didn't seem any happier. "What's wrong now?" I asked Drake.

"Mom, it doesn't matter whether you did the dirty-deed or not; if you have a boyfriend how are you and Dad ever going to get back together?"

"Honey, I don't have a boyfriend, but what makes you think your father wants to get back together?" I asked him.

"He told me."

"I'm afraid it's your dad who has a girlfriend. I met her last night."

"But last night he was with Katie."

"Exactly," I said.

"But Mom, Katie is not Dad's girlfriend. She's his group leader." Drake could tell from the look on my face that I had no idea what kind of a group Katie was leading and Marv was following. "Mom, she's from Dad's Children of Holocaust Survivors group. She's got a Ph.D. in social work or psychology or something and runs this group. It's really helped Dad." This was all news to me.

"Even so, there might be something between them. They've been out together several times," I said.

"I know Katie already has someone in her life."

"But I can't help thinking that a boyfriend or husband would mind if she went out with a male client so much."

"She has someone in her life who doesn't mind at all, and it's not a boyfriend or a husband. It's a wife."

"That explains things," I said under my breath.

"Look Mom, I'm sure this Patrick is a great guy, plus he's young, and I suppose, you might think hot. But don't you realize you have something more with Dad—a shared history not to mention three adorable kids. Are you really ready to give all that up?"

I was looking at Drake, but I wasn't seeing my little boy. I was seeing someone on the verge of adulthood. I assured him that I wouldn't jump into anything with Patrick, and that

I understood Drake wanted me to have a talk with his dad as soon as possible.

"Good. And I understand the only dirty-deed going on here last night was stain removal," he said and gave me a hug. I didn't know whose kid this was, but I wanted to keep him. "And Mom, if you ever walk in late at night and find a hot teenage girl in just a bathrobe, you'll give me a chance to explain, right?"

"Nice try," I said and continued stacking the dishwasher.

Monday morning I got into the office as soon as the kids were off to school. I wanted to get my mind on work. At eleven o'clock Sara informed me that Katherine wanted to see me in her office. I knocked and Katherine yelled, "Enter." She was at her desk doing a crossword puzzle. When she looked up at me, I could see she was wearing a green facial-mask. It had already hardened on her face.

"I heard about your laundry problem. So, how is Drake doing?" She spoke while hardly moving her pursed lips in order to avoid the mask from cracking.

"You'd make an excellent ventriloquist," I told her.

"Exfoliating. I find my life needs exfoliating right now."

"Really?" I grabbed a chair and sat down.

"It's nothing really. Paddy is off on another wild map chase. He located some ancient map in Egypt, and he's gone to buy it. I was going to surprise him and fly home this weekend."

"You could join him in Egypt," I suggested.

"Good Lord, I don't have to see him that badly. I'll wait and maybe have an herbal wrap at the club tonight," Katherine said. If only everyone's problems could be alleviated with spa treatments I thought. "But tell me is Drake all right? I don't want my son traumatizing your son."

"He's fine. I explained everything," I said.

"Good. Patrick is concerned and so am I."

"I think you should know it's beginning to crack."

"What is?" Katherine asked.

"Your face-mask. You should probably rinse now."

"Good Lord, it is getting hot," she said as she hurried to her private bathroom.

I had promised Patrick that I would call him after I spoke to Drake, but I put it off until after I spoke to Katherine. Then I called Patrick, and we met for lunch. We walked over to a little coffee shop near my office, Nachie's Noshery. I didn't want to go anywhere nice or make any big decisions about lunch so Nachie's seemed the place to go. I told Patrick everything Drake had said—how Marv wanted to get back together.

"It's not all up to Marv," Patrick said. "You have a say in this." I knew that was true, but I wasn't sure what I wanted. Here I had this fantastic guy, but I also had a husband who was willing to work things out.

"I have to give Marv a chance," I told Patrick.

"Just as long as you give me a chance too," Patrick said.

"I think you might want to meet someone younger ..."

He interrupted me, "There's no age problem."

I went on, "I didn't mean that I'm too old for you. I know now that's not true. I am thinking about you missing out on having a child. You can say it's not important to you, but what if it becomes important later on? You're always saying you would never name your son Patrick the Fifth. Well, you wouldn't say that if you never thought about it," I told him.

"You said it isn't the age thing."

"It's not. As a matter of fact, I can still have children, but I'm not planning on having any more. Over the past eighteen years I've raised three children and a husband. Now, I want to take care of my family and write novels."

"Linda, I'm not going to let you write me off just yet. If you stopped seeing me today I'd still be childless. I'd be thinking about you, not about meeting fertile, young women in their twenties ..."

"I was thinking more in their mid-thirties," I said.

"Early forties, whatever. The point is, how does your getting back with the husband who left you get me a child?" Patrick was right— getting my marriage back wasn't Patrick's solution—it might be my solution or Marv's solution, but I wasn't even sure of that.

I promised Patrick I would leave things as they were between us. But I also told him I had promised Drake I would talk things over with Marv. That was the next step I had to take.

CHAPTER SEVENTEEN

*D*O *it like you did the last time, when we all thought you looked hot."* That was Drake telling me how to arrange my hair.

"You said I didn't look hot."

"I lied. You looked hot," he said. I continued snipping the ends of my hair.

"Use some of this," said Agatha as she handed me her special hair mousse that no one else was allowed to use. I applied the mousse. It did the trick. My waves moved in all different directions framing my face.

"Wear your cashwear sweater," said Delilah meaning cashmere. "It makes you feel soft like a kitty."

"When you're through with dinner, put the plates in the sink," I told my kids. "And make sure Delilah goes to bed by seven-thirty."

"Right," Agatha said facetiously. It was a family joke, because Delilah had never been to bed before nine-thirty, but seven-thirty was a fantasy goal of mine. That was the hour I knew Delilah's friends went to sleep. I had set out Thai food on the kitchen table.

I put on my gray cashmere, "kitty", sweater—and my gray fluted skirt. I zipped up my black leather boots and finished my make-up. Kissing the kids on my way out, I turned to them and said, "Remember, seven-thirty."

"Right," they all replied, but I knew it would be more like nine o'clock. I left and headed over to meet Marv at our favorite place on Greenbay Road.

Parking on Greenbay was next to impossible, so I pulled onto Central Street. Despite the cold, there were loads of people walking into the many restaurants that dotted the landscape. I figured I'd have to drive a few blocks and pull into the public parking lot, but I got lucky. A space opened up on my right when a silver Suburban pulled out. I was able to slip my van comfortably into the spot.

I could see my breath as I walked briskly to the restaurant. I passed young couples with their arms around each other's waists, middle-aged couples holding hands, and older couples linking arms at the elbows.

"Welcome to Jilly's," Pierre, the maître d', greeted me. "Dr. Mittelman is already here." He led me over to an intimate table in the corner near the window where Marv was seated munching on a breadstick. Marv stood as Pierre pulled out the chair for me.

Most of the tables were filled. The clientele ranged from one young couple in their twenties to a family of three generations. The grandchildren were grown, and the grandparents were an elegant couple in their eighties. Although it was a busy evening at Jilly's, the atmosphere encouraged diners to speak in hushed tones. Still, I sensed an air of celebration and romance in the cozy room.

This was the place where Marv and I had dined for special occasions: birthdays, anniversaries, and other celebrations, and when I thought I was experiencing early menopause, which turned out to be a surprise mid-life pregnancy. Marv had been elated. I had been worried because I had had some drinks the week before and hadn't been taking daily vitamins.

My doctor assured me that it was too early in my pregnancy to make a difference.

Afterwards, I relaxed and walked around with a smirk on my face as if I had some great secret. Suddenly, I noticed all the other pregnant women out there, and recognized I was a senior member of this special club.

Marv and I weren't at Jilly's to celebrate, so what were we here for? "I need to explain some things," Marv said. So, that's what we were here for — explanations.

"You know about Katie?" Marv asked, and I nodded. "She's really doing some incredible work, very talented. Joining her group has helped me understand why I wanted to leave our marriage. I didn't want the kids to suffer the way I had."

"But we're nothing like your folks," I said as I took a forkful of my salad, disrupting the perfect pattern of apples, walnuts, and grated ginger on bits of Savoy cabbage.

"That's true, but still, you know how I would get angry at every little thing, and you would accuse me of being like my dad? Then I would deny it but get angrier inside at myself, because I knew I really was reacting to things just like my father. I didn't want to treat you and the kids the same way my mom and Stuey and I were treated. Turning fifty made me think about it. I felt scared. That's why I left."

I took a sip of my pinot grigio. When I placed the wine glass back on the table, I noticed I had spotted the beautiful white tablecloth with some of my orange and black pepper dressing. I felt a lump in my throat.

"When we were together I hardly noticed how much you criticized me. But once you left, you wouldn't understand this, but it's like when I wear an underwire bra all day and then remove it. All that pressure of the wires digging into me is gone. There's just a sense of relief. That was what it was like. If I made a little mistake, you weren't there to comment on it or to get angry." Maybe it was like removing a pair of really constricting jockey shorts, because Marv looked as if he understood.

It felt good telling him this, like I was removing that

bra once more. I took another sip of pinot grigio. This time I noticed I had dropped a walnut on the tablecloth. When I picked it up and put it on my plate, I could see it left a blotch on the cloth, but now, for some reason, it didn't bother me to see the stain.

Over estouffade of duckling with fresh thyme sauce, Marv explained what he had learned in his Children of Holocaust Survivors group. Over poached Norwegian salmon in a white wine sauce with chives, I listened. Marv had felt a sense of relief to be a part of a group of people with whom he had a shared experience. Growing up, he had always felt different from the other kids at school. They were mostly kids with regular American parents. The other kids homes weren't filled with chaos — screaming, survivor guilt, or occasional nervous breakdowns.

"Katie explained that there were so many survivors who went to Israel. They were there to build a country, and they were together. It was like group therapy for them. But the ones who came here were on their own. Most of them never got any help, which they desperately needed, to cope with their past. Instead, they raised families. There were all kinds of secrets in those houses," Marv said. "At first, I was really angry with my folks, blaming them for all my schtick, but through my group meetings, I began to realize they did the best they could. They were damaged in the war and didn't have the tools to raise us any differently. As an adult, it's now up to me to be the best I can be. I can't blame them any longer." When Marv said that, I could see the whole weight of his childhood lift off his shoulders. He was smiling. "I'm glad I told you this. I feel like…"

"You've taken off a tight underwire bra?" I asked.

"A too small jock strap." Essentially, the same thing.

We ordered dessert. Marv had tea and créme brûlée. I had cappuccino and flourless chocolate cake. "Why flourless?" I asked. "What's the big problem with flour?"

"I think it makes it more fudgy," Marv said.

"I wouldn't mind if they threw in a little flour. I don't see what's the big deal," I said. Marv agreed.

Pierre was bringing a cake over to the table with the large family. It was the grandparents' sixtieth anniversary. You could see the couple still loved each other. They looked as if they understood each other. The adult grandchildren were making toasts to the couple. One of the granddaughters, a beautiful, tall blonde, stood up, raised her glass, and said, "To happy marriages everywhere!"

CHAPTER EIGHTEEN

*T*he *way I see it, you have two men crazy for you ... one's
your husband, the other one's ... not your husband. That's
as good as it gets,"* said Laurie. We were having our morning coffee at the Starbucks in Lincolnwood. *I was having a grande
vanilla-skim-latte, Laurie — a tall skim-latte.*

There was a line to get drinks. The usual morning coffee
drinkers were there: Lana from the alderman's office, two
older Jewish women with their ninety-year-old mother, an
attorney who had once introduced himself to me as Matt, and
Nancy the fine artist, who was always covered with various
colors of oil paint. I'd hung out here many times writing
articles. I got to know people.

The woman I secretly called Mrs. Morrie, entered with
her Starbucks' mug waiting to be filled. She and her husband
own Morrie's House of Chachkes situated on the corner of the
small strip mall on Touhy, which houses the Starbucks. They
live in the apartment over the video store next to Starbucks.
The mall also houses a pet store, Gino's salon, which caters

mostly to older Bubbe types seeking puffy hairdos, a florist shop, Stilettos—a womens shoe store specializing in *come F-me* high heels owned by a couple who look like they were part of the Russian mafia, Jerald Jewelers, The Kleanest Kleaner—the establishment owned by Mrs. Park and Kim, and the office of a Chinese alternative doctor.

I always had to laugh when I would see Mrs. Morrie in the mall. She never had to leave this half-block-long world of hers. She could eat sandwiches, cakes and coffee in Starbucks, have her hair done by Gino (which I knew she did regularly), get flowers, pick out jewelry, bring in her wool clothes for cleaning, buy cat food, rent videos, and have her spine straightened by Dr. Woo without leaving the strip mall. And, if need be, she could cross the busy intersections of Lincoln and Touhy to buy groceries at Lincolnwood Produce or sewing supplies from the fabric store to make her own clothing.

"You see the woman with the bad shaytel?" Laurie asked me.

"Which bad shaytel?" I asked, because two women had walked in together. I knew they were sisters who had a real estate business in the neighborhood—Shvesters Real Estate. They were in their early sixties and big bottomed. They both wore big, dark, fluffy, flip-styled wigs, and they wore too much lipstick.

"The one who looks like Aunt Clara from *Bewitched*." I knew she meant the bigger bottomed of the two. Laurie continued, "I was at the Moscow Tea Room last week, and she was there."

"So?" I asked.

"Well, it's not kosher. She sees me around the neighborhood, you know, at frum functions."

"Well you eat at regular restaurants," I said.

"Yes, but I'm modern Orthodox. I wear pants—never wore a shaytel," she said.

"So because you're frum-lite you can be seen eating *traife* ..."

"I was eating fish," she said.

"Fine," I went on, "and because you're frum-lite you can be seen in non-kosher restaurants."

"Sure, besides, who's seeing me? Civilians. Any frummies who see me aren't supposed to be there themselves. Anyway, she was hiding her face behind a post. She did not want me to see her. When she came in here, I noticed she was avoiding eye contact with me. Now, I think she's afraid I'll tell someone."

"Which you are doing right now," I added.

"But just you. You know you're privy to all the *loshon hora* around here.

Laurie was back to my dilemma, "You're in the perfect situation. Marv's still paying the mortgage. He wants to date you. Patrick wants to date you. I don't see the problem," Laurie said.

"Laurie, just because your situation works for you doesn't mean it's the right thing for me," I said.

"Currently, it's not working for me. I'm not seeing anyone. I even crashed two *shiva* houses last week," she told me.

"Come on."

"Really, my friend Rivka does it all the time. She's always meeting men that way. Just show up with a kugel in hand, say *it's such a loss* to whomever you meet, and the next thing you know, you're being introduced to eligible males. But last week's shiva houses weren't very popular. Next week I'm going with Rivka to a few more. She's going to show me how to do it right."

"Whose shiva houses will you be going to?" I asked her.

"Obviously, I don't have that information yet."

Susan reached me on my cell phone while I was leaving the parking lot of the strip mall. I saw Mrs. Morrie going upstairs to her apartment carrying her coffee mug. *How convenient*—I was thinking.

"I heard from Marv's attorney that he won't be sending over the paperwork," Susan said. "I think that's great."

"Marv wants to work things out," I told her.

"That's the best thing. Do you really want to be out there dating, crashing shiva houses?"

"How do you know about that?" I asked.

"I hear a lot around the office. Even the shiksas are doing it—the ones of a certain age. They figure a Jewish man in his fifties has already raised his kids Jewish, now he can marry out of the faith. Besides, Marv's a great guy."

"There's the matter of Patrick," I told her.

"The Jewish WASP. I'm sure he's wonderful, but you'll just be trading Marv in for a new set of baggage. Everything's great when you're dating, but what do you think things will be like down the road when you're both used to each other, the novelty has worn off, and you're paying bills, picking up each other's garbage, or fighting over the kids? There's little romance when you're plunging the toilet after him," Sue said.

"How do you know he's got intestinal issues?" I asked.

"He's a man, duh. And, do you really want someone new to see you without clothes on?" Sue asked.

"There's always lights out and a silk kimono," I answered. Just then I noticed traffic on Touhy was slowing to a halt. There were cops in the street talking to the drivers. I told Sue I had to hang up.

"Seat belt violation," the officer with his head in my window yelled to the officer behind him, then he instructed me to pull into the parking lot on my right. I pulled in and waited behind a dozen cars. A very good-looking policeman with an Italian name came up to my window.

"Haven't you heard about them cracking down on seat belt violators? I'm really sorry. I mean they're making me do this," Officer Grinelli said. The thing is, I almost always wear my seat belt, but I guess with all the talk about crashing shiva houses and major life changes, I had just forgotten.

"It's okay," I said. "I'm really sorry," I told him. "I

should be wearing my seat belt. You're just doing your job." I was trying to make him feel better. I bet when he joined the force he hoped he'd be solving crimes instead of issuing tickets for seat belt violations. But Officer Grinelli wasn't one of Chicago's Finest, he was one of Lincolnwood's Finest. This was probably the most criminal activity he had ever come across.

"This is so stupid, but I need your drivers license and proof of insurance," he told me.

"No problem," I said as I handed them over.

"Again, I'm really sorry. You'll have to wait a few minutes," he said as he disappeared. The line behind me was getting longer. The drivers in the cars ahead of me were getting tickets from other good-looking officers and then leaving.

"I'm really sorry for issuing you a ticket. The instructions are on the back. Here's your insurance card," he said.

I wanted to get my license back so I asked him, "Can I give you my Triple A card in place of my license."

"Is it one of the good plans?" he asked.

"It's the deluxe family plan," I told him as I traded my Triple A card for my license.

When I got to my office the next day, there was a white orchid plant on my desk. The card read, *Just because.* It was signed *Love, Marv.* There was an e-mail from Patrick telling me he missed me. After my dinner at Jilly's, I had let both men know that I needed time to think and write. I wanted to work on my novel. Taking a little break from romance really helped, and I was able to write the first ten chapters of my book.

"When are you going to let me look at it?" I looked over my shoulder and there was Katherine. She was holding a huge bottle of Pellegrino water.

"Look at what, and what's with the big bottle?" I asked.

"Take a look at your book, and I'm hydrating now."

"How do you know I've got anything for you to read yet?"

"Patrick told me. Come into my office." I followed Katherine. She sat behind her desk. I sat across from her. "Good Lord Linda, I have terrific connections in the publishing industry and with many New York literary agents. I can get you an introduction as soon as you're ready. And don't tell me you want to do this on your own," she said.

"Katherine, I'm not an idiot. I'm also not your child who wants to make it without help from her mom. Of course I'd love you to read it and help me get an agent. Why wouldn't I?" I asked.

"Oh, I don't know. I was just worried. My friend Martin Guberman is a producer in LA. I was just speaking to him, and his son Cary won't let him help him. Cary is a cinematographer, and he won't take any help from his dad. I guess it just got me thinking," Katherine explained.

"Maybe Cary wants to assert his independence. He must have issues with his dad. But I don't. I'll even let Martin Guberman help if it makes him feel any better."

"Excellent. So, when can I read it?" she asked. I explained I was stuck on the eleventh chapter, but I would let her read the entire first draft once I had it.

"I'm looking forward to it. Oh, I almost forgot. This is for you." Katherine handed me an envelope with my name on it. "Someone brought it in this morning. Is there a dancing messenger service in town?" I shrugged and took it to my desk.

The envelope contained a glossy flier for Philip Pfeffer's exhibit of Jewish wedding photos at the Spertus Museum. There was a sticky note with his phone number requesting that I call him. I figured he was hoping I'd write about it. I gave him a call.

An exuberant female receptionist answered. "Philip Pfeffer Photography, make all your dreams photographic. May I help you.?"

"Is Philip there?" I asked.

"Who may I say is calling?"

"This is Linda Grey. He asked that I call."

"So you're returning his call?" she asked.

"He hasn't called, but he wants me to call him," I explained.

"I'm going to put you on hold," she said without her former exuberance.

"Linda, it's Phil Pfeffer. I was near your office, so I stopped in. I thought you might be interested in seeing my exhibit." I told him that although I would be interested, I was busy all week, but I might be downtown soon and would stop in.

"I don't want you to stop in. I want to bring you. We could go to dinner first. Like a date," he said.

"A date?"

"I figured you and Dr. Mittelman are no longer together, so why not?" he asked.

"I'm not available to date. And, if I do date, it'll be my husband or my boyfriend," I explained.

On my way home from the office, I started to think how crazy it was that Marv wanted to get back with me, Patrick wanted to have a relationship with me, and now this pirouetting photographer was interested. But I didn't want any more complications. I wanted to write.

That evening I put Delilah to bed as usual, and (as usual) I fell asleep in bed with her. I awoke at 3:00 AM and decided to get some more writing done. I had left my laptop in the kitchen. Agatha was instant-messaging friends on my computer while Drake was making himself some macaroni and cheese. "What are you doing up so late?" I asked them.

"Mom, we're always up at this time of night," Agatha told me.

I knew that Marv had always stayed up late on the computer doing his medical billing, but I was completely unaware that I was living with adolescent bats. It had always been difficult to wake them for school, but I thought that was just their teenage nature. I had no idea they were living this nocturnal existence.

"You both need to go to sleep right now," I insisted.

"It's okay Mom, we'll make up for it on the weekend," Agatha said.

"Dad always stayed up with us when he was living here," Drake said.

"Well, it's just me now, so get to bed."

"I miss Dad," Drake said as he went to his room.

"You too," I said to Agatha.

"Okay. I'm just signing off." She was writing something in that teenage instant-messaging code that probably meant *Mom's a loser*.

So, they had special times together while I was sleeping. There was a whole night-time world going on in my house that I didn't know about. My kitchen was some kind of modern speakeasy. In place of moonshine, there was all night mac and cheese. In place of girlie shows, there was instant-messaging. And in place of money laundering, there was medical billing. Marv was Bugsy Siegal. I was Elliot Ness. I had run the illicit activity out of town, at least for the night. I settled into my novel.

Chapter Nineteen

*W*hen *the first promise of spring appears in Chicago it brings with it a new attitude in the residents of the city. People are out walking. They smile when they pass each other. Strangers comment, "Nice day." The snow thaws, the temperature rises, and folks know they have achieved something – they have survived another winter.*

Although they won't say it, Chicagoans have little respect for those who live in mild climates year round. After all, what have those folks achieved come May – just months and months of beautiful weather. Midwest living is not for sissies. So, on the first nice day, there is a feeling of pride and accomplishment in the air. It is, however, a false feeling, because winter will usually rear it's ugly head at least a few times before summer arrives. The truth is, there is no real spring season in Chicago, just an occasional nice day, then more cold, lots of rain, possible snow showers, and some hail until the ninety-five percent humidity and ninety-eight degree weather shows up. But, when that first nice day arrives the city comes alive, you can feel the pulse of it's people. It is a magical moment.

That first nice day in April, I found myself compelled to walk and walk. The sun was shining. I could smell new plants bursting through the earth. I had gotten halfway through my novel. I needed to talk to an expert in the field of children of Holocaust survivors. Marv had given me Katie's phone number. We met for coffee at Borders on Michigan Avenue. I gave her some of my pages which she read. Katie told me I was on the right track. She gave me some pointers on the types of emotional problems that tend to crop up. I took notes. She had to leave for an appointment. I walked out on Michigan Avenue, and before I knew it, I was outside the Spertus Museum. I remembered the photography exhibit so I walked in. Philip Pfeffer was one of several photographers whose wedding photos were being showcased. There were several small groups of people looking around as well as a few individuals.

Pictures of *ketuba* signings, pictures of brides performing the custom of circling the groom seven times, pictures of sweet tables and more lined the walls, but it was the display of photographs of the groom stepping on the glass that caught my eye.

The flying shards reflecting prisms of light while guests shielded their eyes—this was the photo that brought that evening back to me. The photo was both spectacular and grotesque—spectacular in it's display of flying glass and grotesque in the contorted frightened faces of the guests.

Viewing all the other photos lining the walls gave me a rare glimpse into the marriage of strangers but seeing photos of Lillian's wedding brought that evening back into focus. There was a picture of Patrick and me dancing. My head was pressed against his chest. I could recall the scent of cinnamon, wood chips, and merlot. There was a photo of Marv dipping me on the dance floor and reeking of charm. It was reminiscent of that *Life* magazine photo I'd seen of celebrants dancing in the streets on D-Day.

There was the photograph of the guests lifting the newly

wed couple into the air on chairs. Philip completely captured the horror on Lillian's face when she was being carried on the chair. And there was the photo of Barry in mid-air on his way down to the floor.

"Linda, hi. Isn't it something?" The words came from a tall, slender, stunning woman in a pink, wool slack suit. She looked familiar, but I could not figure out who she was. Yet, she seemed to know me.

"What?" I was trying to buy time to figure this out.

"The photograph," she said.

"Oh, yes. Something. You should have been there," I said.

"But I was there," she remarked. I'd heard that voice before. "Linda, it's Millie." I must have looked confused. "I don't blame you for not recognizing me," she went on, "I finally did it." Millie had fixed her nose.

We walked through the exhibit together, and Millie explained to me why she had waited so long to alter her profile. As a child her parents hoped she'd grow into her nose. Then when she was grown, she was too busy in college studying and attaining her advance degrees.

In the working world, her success in her field was based on her keen sense of taste. She consulted with plastic surgeons, but none of them could guarantee that her sense of smell and taste wouldn't be affected. Then recently, she heard of a doctor doing wonderful things with lasers. He promised her that her sense of smell, and hence taste, would not change.

"So was the doctor right? Was your sense of smell or taste altered?"

"Actually, it was affected but for the better. My sense of smell is even keener now. Probably due to my not having all that extra flesh in the way," Millie explained.

"Wow, Millie, you're a knockout," I told her.

"I know. Look at me," she said smiling. Then she took a compact and lipstick out of her purse. The compact was silver with a silver test-tube on the top. Millie opened it and applied salmon-colored lipstick.

"I love wearing lipstick now," she said. I asked her if that was a miniature test-tube on the case; she told me that it was, and that Walt had it designed especially for her. Then she turned it over and read the inscription, "Always Millie, always beautiful, always Walt." Always the gentleman, I thought. Walt had been coming into Chicago on the weekends to see Millie. It had gotten pretty serious between the two of them.

"But, I'm not getting married," Millie said.

"Why not?" I asked.

"I've been there already — twice. I have my career, friends. I'm past having children. Of course, with technology or adoption I could still have them, but I'm past wanting any. I really care for Walt. I'm enjoying things the way they are." It was clear Millie did not need a husband to define herself as a woman.

"How is your project coming along?" I asked.

"It's very close to fruition," she said.

"You mean the fat-free frying oil?" I sounded like I was practicing a tongue-twister.

"Yes. The hardest part has been saying *fat-free frying oil*," she said.

Later that evening, I sat down at the kitchen table wearing my bathrobe and pink straw hat.

"Mom, I'm hungry," Drake said. I waved him away.

"Come on Mom. You're still our mother," said Agatha.

"You know the rule," I said.

"Just heat up a pizza, please, Mom. I love you," said Drake.

"You can read the instructions on the box. That's all I'm saying because I'm not here," I said.

"You have to take care of us and nuture us. We didn't ask to be born," said Agatha.

"That's right. Why should we suffer just because you and Dad had a careless momentary indiscretion," Drake added.

"You were planned," I said.

I had instituted the rule a week earlier. The rule was

when I'm wearing my pink straw hat, I'm Linda Grey the novelist at work. When I take the hat off, I'm Mom. I had given the kids dinner, cleaned up, and put Delilah to bed by laying down with her. We both fell asleep, but I awoke after fifteen minutes and went straight to my writing. Agatha and Drake were hovering nearby.

"You're supposed to nurture us," Agatha said.

"I don't nurture after 10:00 PM," I told her. "You can both go to your rooms and try to get to bed by a decent hour for a change."

"Not only are we a product of a broken home, but now we're neglected," Drake said to Agatha as he headed to his room.

"I'm going to call the ASPCA," Agatha said on her way to her room.

"You mean DCFS," Drake shouted as he closed his door.

Left to my work, I was really enjoying writing. I always liked writing my columns, but they were short pieces and didn't take me away from my everyday world. This was different. I got to know my characters. I began to live among them when I was at the keyboard. I could get involved in their lives and leave my world temporarily. But the writing soon became a drug. Like the heroin addict, I looked forward to my escape everyday. I even enjoyed preparing my paraphernalia the way, I supposed, an addict enjoyed gathering up his spoon, lighter, hypodermic needle, and rubber hose. I would clear off the kitchen table, then set up my laptop, a cup of tea, and usually find a pair of readers to place on the table. I would put on my writer's hat, sit down, open my laptop, and delve into the world I had created.

I could control my characters' actions. I still did what I had to do around the house: driving the kids places they had to be, helping them with homework, but as far as my personal life went, that was consumed with my craft.

One morning, after all the kids were off to school, I opened my laptop. There was a knock on the door. It was Marv with a potted African violet and a cappuccino.

"I thought you might like a cappuccino and a little bit of springtime to help you write," Marv told me as he handed me what he'd brought. "I'm not going to bother you. Have a great day." He gave me a peck on the cheek, and left.

I started to remember how sweet he could be. I remembered when we went to Agatha's school conference last year. All the teachers sat at desks in the gymnasium. We went from one teacher to the next getting favorable reports on Agatha. I wanted to leave, but we hadn't spoken to the gym teacher. All my kids are natural athletes and in good shape, so I figured we could skip that report. Besides, I had to get back to the office, but Marv insisted we talk to Mr. Starck.

"I noticed he's been sitting all alone the whole time we've been here," Marv had said. "Most of the parents don't take physical education seriously. He looks so sad." So, Marv dragged me over to Mr. Starck's desk.

"We're Agatha's parents," Marv told Mr. Starck, who then preceded to look up Agatha's scores on her sit-ups, push-ups, sprints, etc.

"Most of the parents don't even bother to find out how their children are doing in physical education. They don't think it's important," Starck told us.

"Well, we feel it's very important," Marv had said. I had nodded in agreement, and we both thanked the P.E. teacher who had suddenly sprouted a smile on his face. I remembered Marv and I had both felt good leaving the conferences. We had done a *mitzvah*, boosting Mr. Starck's morale. I also felt proud that I had such a thoughtful, caring husband.

However, later that evening Marv had demonized me for leaving the peanut butter jar out on the kitchen counter with it's lid off. That was Marv—doing wonderful things for others while harping on those closest to him for minor infractions.

I wrote, drank the cappuccino, and admired the African violet. Later I went into my office and found a surprise at my desk. A small box of four Godiva dark chocolate truffles had been placed next to my phone. The card read *To keep up your strength. Love, Patrick.*

I'd only known Patrick for a short time. He'd been sweet, thoughtful, and romantic. I couldn't help wondering had we a long history would there be disappointing moments? Would he have shown me another side—his short tempered side? Would I be eating these chocolates and alternating between both good and bad stories of him? After all, the truffles were bittersweet.

A strange thing happens to procrastinators. They tend to get everything accomplished except what they intend to get done. And so it was with me. I wanted to finish my book, but halfway through, writer's block set in. At home I would sit in front of my laptop, but I found myself getting up, organizing drawers, straightening closets, and recycling magazines.

I came across several Israel Bonds that were Chanukah gifts to my children. I had intended to bring them into my safety deposit box in the bank's vault but hadn't been there in over a year. I would usually do my banking at a branch drive-thru. This instance required me to go to the main branch in Lincolnwood.

I gathered the bonds and drove to the bank, but when I got to the main branch, the bank wasn't there. The building was missing! I drove around the block. It still wasn't there. Had I imagined that the main branch of my bank had stood there all these years? I felt like I was in an episode of *The Twilight Zone*. My heart began racing faster. I was confused and shaken. The world, as I knew it, could not exist if a person's bank fell off the face of the earth.

I drove to the branch drive-thru a mile away. I pressed the talk button. With panic in my voice, I asked what had happened to the main branch and was told it was torn down. The items in my safety deposit box began floating around in my mind: Israel bonds, US savings bonds, my grandmother's jewelry, my children's baby hospital-identification wristbands, birth certificates, passports, my college diary. I didn't want to lose these things, and I didn't want the diary to fall into the wrong hands.

"But what about my things in the vault?" I shouted into the drive-thru speaker. The teller informed me they had been moved to the temporary trailer in the parking lot. She instructed me to drive back and go across the street to the bank parking lot.

I was releived but still shaking as I drove back to the location of the main branch. I noticed there was a trailer in the lot and went into it. It was set up like a mini-bank. There were desks and bankers and counters and tellers. I signed a card, and the guard, an old man, let me into the vault. I placed the bonds into my box. On the way out, I asked, "Is it safe?"

The guard told me, "It's safer than the old building." That, I had gathered. After all, at least the trailer was still standing.

CHAPTER TWENTY

*J*UST *let me see what you have so far,"* Katherine pleaded. *She had been relentless over the past week, so I took the 156 pages which were in my briefcase and handed them to her. "Good Lord Linda, you've written this much? Why it's practically finished!"*

"Not really. The characters need to tie up some loose ends in their lives. I'm a little stuck at the moment," I told her.

"That elusive animal—writer's block. It's a monster. Keeps you up at night cleaning the kitchen, scrubbing floors, doing everything but writing." So, Katherine had also been there. "When I was writing erotica for a romance line—don't look so surprised, this was years ago—if I'd get blocked, Paddy would know it, because, although we had a housekeeper, I'd be polishing the silverware after she'd already done it. When I was working on my series of biblical erotica, I vacuumed the foyer so much, we had to replace the carpeting, and it was only two years old. But I finally finished *The Loins of Moses,*" she said.

"I know that book. Are you telling me you wrote *The Loins of Moses?*" I asked.

"Mostly," she said. "I have to give Paddy credit. He helped me in spots whenever I hit a snag. He developed the desert maps in the book."

"Are you saying you're ..."

"Romana Roman," Katherine finished my sentence. "I kept it a secret for years. That was Paddy's idea. He comes from a very WASPY New England clan. To be honest, they were a bunch of stiffs. The older generation is all gone now. I don't think they ever approved of me anyway. It really doesn't matter anymore who knows. I just hadn't thought about that part of my career in a long time. But I loved writing novels. That's why I'm so excited for you, and I can't wait to read this tonight," she said, waving my manuscript.

I could not get over the fact that Katherine was Romana Roman. In my sophomore year of high school my friend Leslie Fried had snuck a copy of *The Loins of Moses* to me in Mrs. Heineman's English class. I read it on my lap at my desk in Señora Epstein's Spanish class for the next two weeks and wound up with a *D* in Spanish.

Then, at the University of Illinois, Marty Goldman insisted on reading passages to me late at night in the lounge of the Sigma Alpha Mu fraternity house. Marty kept trying to grope me at the end of each chapter. Romana Roman's descriptions of the Hebrews' sexual escapades were so poetic and lyrical that by the end of chapter six he succeeded.

Later, I went to pick up Delilah from her Brownie meeting at the JCC. I parked in the lot and ran into the building still thinking about Romana Roman and *The Loins of Moses*. I collected Delilah and her backpack. When I got back to my car in the parking lot, I noticed my driver's side window was smashed. At first it seemed surreal to me—standing there, window smashed, with shards of broken glass all over. Then I realized I had left my purse in the car with all the its contents. I felt sick. I felt violated. I was in shock.

Suddenly, it hit me—this was all really happening. I was standing with Delilah, a broken window, and a missing purse. I needed to take action. I remembered my cell phone had fallen under the passenger seat while I had been driving. I checked and luckily, it was still there. I called the 24th district police.

I had written an article stressing the importance of making photocopies of everything in one's wallet, but I had failed to follow my own advice. Now I had to try to remember all the things I had kept in my purse. I called my credit card company. When I gave the man at the other end my name, he said in a nasal voice, "We've just cancelled your credit card. It may have been stolen."

"How did you know?" I asked.

"Are you a tall, burly, white male in your twenties with a buzz-cut?"

"No," I answered.

"I didn't think so. You have a photo credit card. Someone was just at a Target store in Evanston attempting to make a purchase with your card. The cashier noticed your photo and took your card from the man."

"Did they arrest him. He has my purse, my ID," I said frantically.

"I think he just left," he said. "We're sending you another card with a new account number."

"You the lady who called the police?" a petite brunette officer, who had just arrived on the scene, asked me. She explained to me that there have been several car break-ins at schools and community centers because moms often run into the building locking their purse in the car. "Thieves watch for moms getting out of their cars not carrying a purse," Officer Rodriguez explained.

She wanted to know what kind of purse I had. I told her it was a tan Coach bag. She asked me what kind of a wallet I had. I told her, "A Prada, a fake Prada." Then I wondered if I could get into trouble for having a knockoff designer item, even though it had been a gift from Caro.

The officer must have read my mind. "Don't worry about it. If we arrested everyone with a fake designer piece, eighty percent of the women on the North Shore would be under indictment." I thanked Officer Rodriguez. She handed me a copy of my report, and left.

Once I got home, I made more phone calls. I called Target and spoke to the cashier who had recovered my card. It was the same young kid who sounded like Richard Crenna's character. He told me, with his teenage voice croaking and warbling, that when he confiscated my stolen card, the thief left. I asked the cashier why they didn't detain the man. "I may just be a cashier at Target, but I still think my life is worth living," was his answer.

I called my bank. My checkbook was in my purse, so they closed out my checking account and opened a new account for me. I had never taken my security box key out of my purse, so they transferred me to the vault desk. I recognized the voice of the old guard who worked there. I told him to make a note on my file not to let anyone into my box, because my purse had been stolen, and someone might show up with the key and my drivers license.

It was such a hassle taking care of the little details that are required when someone steals your purse. On top of that, I felt confused because I didn't really know what was in the purse when it had been taken. I felt violated knowing that someone was leafing through my life. I hoped they would just take my cash and credit card, throw the rest away, and that someone would find the purse and return it to me. But would there be any identification left in my purse?

Rationally, I understood this was just an incident of a stolen purse. It should have registered as a mere inconvenience, but somehow, it both angered and saddened me. Of course, I was angry at the thief and at myself for leaving my purse in the car. But I was feeling low from the loss of whatever might have been in my bag.

I didn't want a thief looking at pictures of my kids. Luckily, I had failed to update the family photos I carried, so the thieves would have to go to the police to use that age-enhancement technique (used on the flyers of missing children) just to figure out what my kids would look like at their present ages.

The next few days were taken up with the all necessary little details. I had to notify all the accounts that were paid directly from my checking account or credit card. I had to get a new drivers license.

Then I got a phone call at my office. "Are you Linda Grey?" said a woman's voice.

"Yes," I answered.

"My name is Chaya Malka Solomon. I have some of your things. My son found them in the mud near our house."

"Oh, Chaya Malka, that's such good news," I said and meant it. Chaya Malka explained how she recognized my name from the newspaper and was afraid I'd been mugged or something even more terrible. She was relieved to learn that I was safe.

I had been upset by the loss of my personal items, but when I got the call from Chaya Malka, I felt better. Here was a stranger who took the time to find me. She lived near the JCC, not far from my house. I left the office and headed to Chaya Malka's home.

I parked my car on the street and approached the Solomon home. It was a small, shabby, brick tract house from the fifties. The walkway to the front door was cracked, and the two steps up to the door were sagging and chipped. The front door, which was in need of paint, had a sticker on it that read *This house protected by Chapman Security.*

I knocked on the door. A tall, thin, gangly, haggard-looking woman of an indeterminate age opened the door. She wore a terry-cloth, turban-style head-covering, plain blue, long-sleeved blouse, and a long, baggy cotton skirt. Chaya Malka introduced herself and let me into her foyer. Inside, the house was in even poorer condition. The walls were in need of replastering, the carpeting was worn through, and the meager furniture looked as if it had been provided by the Salvation Army.

A boy about eleven sat at a card table in the dining room reading a Hebrew prayer book. Chaya Malka explained that the boy at the table, Shlomi Moishe, found my things. He looked up from his book to wave to me. Chaya Malka went over to a particleboard bookcase filled with Hebrew books. There was a Ziplock plastic bag on a shelf which she gave me. I thanked her and Shlomi Moishe, and left.

Once I got into my car, I opened the bag. There was my Lifetime Fitness card, some muddied pictures of my kids at a much younger age, my health insurance card, and several store gift cards which I had forgotten about.

I knew this neighborhood was mixed economically. The very religious Jews have to live here, so they can walk to their shuls. When many of them grow prosperous, they do not move out of the neighborhood. They just build bigger houses. When families fall onto hard times, they don't move out to cheaper neighborhoods, they find an apartment, a smaller house, or move in with family. And so, there are people of immense means living among poor families, many of whom get assistance from Jewish agencies.

Seeing the poverty that Chaya Malka lived in, I had been tempted to offer her a reward. But I didn't want to insult her. She had done a mitzvah, so no reward was expected. I would have been happy to have any of my things returned to me, and here I had over $200 worth of gift cards. I remembered noticing a new kosher gourmet store had recently opened on Devon Avenue, A Schtickle Naches. I headed over to see what they had to sell.

The store was filled with all kinds of culinary food items. I picked out a pretty wicker basket and filled it with cookies, pretzels, nuts, jams, dried beans, and dried fruits. The salesgirl wrapped the basket in orange cellophane and attached a big blue bow. I filled out a card, once again thanking Chaya Malka and Shlomi Moishe for being so considerate. They would get the delivery from A Schtickle Naches the next morning.

Even with Marv out of the house, my dining room table was always a mess. Before he moved out there were his patient charts and all kinds of papers spread out on the table. Now, the table was covered with my papers, mail, bills, the kids homework, and an assortment of forms that needed to be filled out. From far away the papers seemed to resemble a lace tablecloth, but as soon as I got closer, my table just looked like the mess it usually is.

While searching for some bills I would need to pay with my new checks, I discovered some job applications. They were from several stores at the local malls. I wasn't sure if Drake, with his heavy school load, had enough free time to take on a job before summer vacation. I made a mental note to discuss this with him. I found the bills and realized they were almost overdue, so I called the bank to inquire about my new checks. I was told they hadn't arrived, but I could come in to get some temporary ones for my new account.

Later at dinner I said to Drake, "Do you think you should start working during this busy semester?"

"No I don't," was his reply.

"Good, then I'll throw out those applications."

Drake looked at me as if I was speaking a foreign language, and Agatha said, "I need those."

"You?" I asked.

"Yes, I want to get a job for the summer," Agatha told me.

"But you're not fifteen yet," I said.

"Mrs. Floman told us at school she could get us work permits. But I need my birth certificate."

I was surprised that it was Agatha looking to apply for a job. But I wasn't against the notion. After all, this would be for summer break. Maybe she'd get up before 3:00 PM. I promised her I would get her birth certificate out of the bank vault as soon as I got my new drivers license from the Secretary of State's Driving facility, and I was going to do that the very next day.

The next morning, I got to the drivers facility early. Even though I was just replacing my stolen license, I still had to wait in line. I got there just as it opened, and the line was still small. I remembered going to renew my license when Delilah was just a baby. She and Agatha had come with me. Delilah was in her stroller, and Agatha stood beside me.

The line was extremely long, and Delilah had gotten fussy so I picked her up. Agatha was tired of standing, so she sat in the baby's stroller. I waited in line holding the baby pushing Agatha, who was about nine years old. There were about twenty people in line ahead of me. Someone from the facility came up to me and moved us to a new line she had just formed with me first. Behind me, she put two other people, both of whom appeared disabled. From there, I moved very quickly through the process.

On my way out, I noticed the original line I had been in had hardly moved at all. I couldn't imagine why I had been pushed ahead. I was tired of holding the baby, and told Agatha to get out of the baby's stroller. Then I realized that Agatha, at nine years old sitting in a stroller, looked as if she could be a disabled child. Someone thought I was holding a baby and pushing a disabled child, and they wanted to help me out. A stroller is not a wheelchair, but the drivers facility employee didn't make that distinction. I explained my theory to Agatha, and after that, whenever we had to wait in lines, she would offer to sit in the baby's stroller.

This time I didn't need a gimmick to move through the line. I got my license just before the place started to get really crowded. I was meeting Marv at Starbucks before going to the bank. He had the other copy of the vault key.

"You should have called me when it happened. I could have helped you with all those calls or taken your van over to the lot for you," Marv said. He was sitting in one of the brown velveteen easy chairs at Starbucks. I sat in the other easy chair. Delilah calls those the cozy chairs, and I always think they're the best place in the store to sit.

Marv was being sweet and helpful, but there wasn't really anything else he could do to make me feel any better. I had been left with a lingering residue of being violated, as if some invader had been privy to my most intimate secrets. I was always scrawling notes to myself on little scraps of paper and shoving them into my purse. Who knows what tidbits were floating around my Coach bag? Marv gave me his copy of the deposit box key and offered to escort me to the bank. I turned down his offer. I had promised myself I wasn't going to be seeing Marv or Patrick until my book was completed. I was just supposed to keep in touch and keep both of them posted on my progress.

I got to the bank, or should I say trailer, and approached a teller. I had my new drivers license, and the teller handed me some temporary checks for my new account. Then I walked down the hall in the trailer to the vault where that same old guard was seated. I informed him that I wanted to visit my box. He asked my name, I told him, and then he pulled my card from the file box.

"There's a note on your card that says, if you come in with ID to get into your box, not to let you."

"I know, that's because when my purse was stolen, someone had my ID and key, but now I have a new drivers license and my second key, so you can let me in," I told him.

"Sorry, these are my instructions," he said, waving the card with the note paper clipped to it.

I went out into the parking lot, sat in my car, and called the bank. I asked to be connected to the safety deposit desk. The old man got on the phone. "This is Linda Grey. I had called a few days ago to request that you don't let me into the vault. You can take that request off of my card now," I said.

I walked back into the trailer/bank. I told the old man I wished to visit my box. So once again he asked my name, pulled my card (which no longer had the note attached to it), asked for my ID, and this time let me in. When I was done, I traded my box for a different one and got new keys. Someone who didn't look anything like me was still out there with my ID and key. I wasn't trusting my stuff to the old man running the vault.

On my way home from the bank with Agatha's birth certificate, I was thinking about the jewelry I kept in the box. When I was in the trailer/bank looking at all my treasures, I didn't see my diamond engagement ring. I thought I had placed it in the box when I was pregnant with Delilah, because my fingers were expanding at the same rate as my uterus. I didn't remember ever taking the ring out of the vault. Now, I was wondering if I had kept it at home all this time in my top dresser drawer, where I keep miscellaneous jewelry.

I was anxious to get home to check. Then I remembered,

I had given a box of things to Marv when he moved into his own apartment. The box had contained mostly Marv's things: cuff links, watches, an antique stick pin, but I had also included my daughter-in-law bracelet.

The daughter-in-law bracelet was the tri-color gold bracelet that Marv's mother, Silke, bought while vacationing in Israel when her sons were teens. She bought two bracelets hoping to give one to each daughter-in-law when her sons married. I got mine, but since Marv's brother had secretly married, Silke still had the second bracelet. Silke continued harboring hopes that one day she could give the other bracelet away to Stuey's bride. Little did she know that the bracelet had a rightful wrist in Milwaukee, and one that would show off it's tri-color in brilliant contrast.

I figured the ring was at home or with Marv. I had to stop in my office before going home, so I tried not to think about it. As I was finishing my latest column, one on American married women's lack of sex drive, I got a call from Marv. He wanted to know how things went at the bank and if I found Agatha's birth certificate. I told him I had found it, but I was concerned because I didn't see my engagement ring in the box.

"Sweetheart, don't worry about it. You most likely have it at home," he told me. I agreed but mentioned that I might have put it in the wooden box I gave him with his jewelry.

"Then it's somewhere and you'll find it," he said in a calming manner. "Linda don't get yourself all worked up."

"I guess I'm stressed after my purse was stolen, and now I wonder where I put the ring," I told Marv.

"Stress is part of life. Everyone has things go wrong sometime. The only way to avoid stress is to move into a nursing home where everything is taken care of for you," Marv told me.

"At least that's something to look forward to," I said jokingly.

"Really, don't worry about it. You'll find the ring. Anyway, it's insured." Marv used to be the one to get upset over every little thing. Now, he had changed. He seemed so logical, rational, and strong. I was feeling anxious about little things. But Marv was right. The ring was most likely at home.

When I got home, Agatha was anxiously awaiting. "Did you find my birth certificate?" she asked rubbing her hands together like an excited fly.

"I have it," I said handing it over to her.

She grabbed it and said, "Yay, I have my birth certificate."

Delilah joined us in the living room. "I want a birth-tificate too," Delilah said.

"It's *cer*tificate, Loser-ella," Agatha said on her way up to her room.

"Don't worry darling," I told Delilah, "you have a birth certificate. I'll show it to you the next time I go to the bank."

Delilah ran towards Agatha's room and yelled, "I knew I was born, too!"

CHAPTER TWENTY-ONE

I *was staring at Katherine's pin – the one Patrick had given her, which was a replica of the Northside News' front page.* *"Good Lord Linda, are you even listening to me?" Katherine's voice pulled me out of my dream-state.*

"Sorry," I said.

"Did you hear what I said about Barbara Crompton?"

"I was up all night looking for something. I'm just a little tired," I said.

"Good Lord, I would think this news would perk you up."

"I guess I wasn't listening. Tell me again," I asked.

"I was, not surprisingly, impressed with your manuscript." Katherine stopped me before I could interrupt her. "I know, it's not finished. Still, what you have is quite good. So I took the liberty to contact Barbara Crompton of the Barbara Crompton Literary Agency in New York. It was nice to catch up with her—we haven't seen each other in ages. Anyway, now I have Barbara interested. She wants you to send her your first three chapters."

This news definitely got my attention and woke me out of my grogginess. So I stopped brooding over the missing ring and turned my attention to completing my book. I thanked Katherine, and as I made my way out of her office she stopped me.

"Did you find what you were looking for last night?"

"No, but it'll show up. I was worried about something, but now I really need to get moving on my book."

I wrote whenever I had a free moment and even when I didn't. I didn't want this to take time away from the kids. I found ways to write and be with them. I would sit with Delilah while she watched a video, and I would write on my laptop mentally blocking out the antics of Pumba and Timon in *The Lion King*.

I wrote while Agatha and I painted our toenails. I would add a paragraph here and there while I prepared a sandwich for Drake. He insisted my sandwiches turned out better than his, but I couldn't recall Drake ever constructing any.

I still wanted to find that ring. When I told Marv about Barbara Crompton he was thrilled for me. He also said he thought he had the ring in that box, but the box was on one of the high shelves in his closet, buried under a mess, and he hadn't had time to get to it. I asked him to check. He said, if it wasn't there, he would let me know. Patrick was equally thrilled for me. Both men agreed with me that I needed to finish the book, and they were willing to give me time and space. This was what I needed.

I had to get deeper into my characters to finish the story. It took a lot of contemplation in the tub, as well as late-night cups of a French-roast, full-bodied blend of coffee. I sent the first three chapters to the Barbara Crompton Literary Agency and got a call from Barbara herself.

"Linda, I'm so glad Katherine told me about you." Barbara sounded enthusiastic. "I haven't yet come across a manuscript about the effects of the Holocaust on the second generation. It's funny and has heart. How soon can you get me the completed novel?" I told her she would most likely have it in a week.

My protagonist Fran Bluestein and her brother Glenn would have to find a way to break the news of Glenn's homosexuality to their parents. Their father Sy was a boastful, narcissistic man who was always bragging to his friends (whose children had married gentiles) that his children would never dare marry out of the faith, because they have too much respect for him.

I had laid the foundations for these personalities, but now I had to conclude the story. Would Glenn's coming out kill his parents, alienate them from him, or would they embrace his partner? Would their parents each have a different reaction, or would they unite in their behavior?

They both had spent time in concentration camps, however, they had come through their experiences differently. They each had employed different techniques to survive. Yet, both were still suffering from post-traumatic-stress syndrome. Even Glenn and Fran displayed signs of this syndrome.

Fran and Glenn confronted their parents one at a time. Their mother, Sylvia, was accepting and even relieved that Glenn had a personal life and could commit to someone, even if it was another man. Sy, at first, took this news as a personal affront. He brooded, he pouted, he considered sitting shiva. Sy felt this was the worst of times, even worse than the dark days in Europe. Slowly, he realized that if he could live through his hellish experiences and could adapt to life in America as a stranger in a strange land, he could also overcome this disappointment.

Day by day the family came together. Glenn brought his friend home to his family. Sy said that he didn't have to like the situation, but he would accept it. And the good news, Glenn's partner, Ross, was Jewish and a doctor.

I hooked up my laptop to the printer in the family room. Sitting in the rocking chair I had used to nurse my children, a Stoly-vanilla-rocks in hand, I sat and watched as the printer spewed out my completed book.

"I finally reach you." It was Jen on the phone. I explained how I had been busy finishing my book and hadn't been answering most calls. Jen just wanted to know if I could drive my van to Lake Geneva, because her kids wanted her to leave her van for their use.

"Also, I spoke to everyone else about this. The resort has a special package, and we can stay for five nights for the same price. I know it's harder for you having a little kid and all, but we all want to stay the extra day." I told Jen I could stay the extra night, and if I needed to do some rewriting on the book, I would have my laptop.

"I think this is so great that you've been writing your dream. When the kids were little I used to make up bedtime stories. I've always wanted to write them down and submit them to publishers, but whenever I would have time to sit down and write, I'd notice a stack of magazines that needed sorting or couch pillows that needed straightening. I just can't concentrate on writing if anything in the house needs work. But you're fantastic with discipline about writing. I know you'll be a great novelist. I once read about the woman who wrote Peyton Place. She never cleaned her house and hardly fed her kids, but she was really motivated to write and wrote a big hit. I just know you'll be a big success," said Jen.

"I hope so, but do you think my house is messy enough and my kids undernourished enough?" I asked her.

"Linda, I didn't mean that. It's just that I'm so organized I never have time to try something new. You know, there are days when I just want to pull those paper clips out of my date book and let the chips, or clips, fall as they may," she told me. "Sometimes I consider not answering my cell phone when it rings. And I know it's one of the kids or Albert. Can you imagine?"

I couldn't. But I didn't to want to sit around trying to imagine Jen ignoring her cell phone ring that played *Battle Hymn of the Republic*." I had to get to the post office to mail my manuscript to, hopefully my new best friend, Barbara Crompton.

The woman looked familiar to me — like I had known her in a previous life. She was waiting in line at Starbucks. Then, three women, who seemed to be her friends, joined her. The three women were quite diverse: one being in her thirties, pudgy and Asian; one being sixty-ish and bi-racial; and the third, a tiny, mousy blonde. But the woman who looked familiar was just about my age. Her dark, wavy hair was short and stylish.

I was sitting on one of the cozy chairs. Since I had just mailed Barbara the hopes and dreams for my future, I decided to treat myself to something sweet and gooey — a tall caramel-machiato with whipped cream. I now considered myself a real novelist and felt it was my duty to observe strangers in public settings (although I had always done this out of nosy curiosity). So here I was, observing.

I asked myself again, who is this woman? I tried tuning out all the other voices in the room, so I could hear her talk. She was telling her friends about some difficulty she was having with her boss — something to do with spreadsheets or data. I couldn't really follow the context of her speech, but I was listening to the timbre of her voice. It was deep and low and felt familiar.

I tried to concentrate on the sound. I could only recall two women I'd known with such voices — Lucy Byron, a girl I knew slightly in college, and Judy Hudnut, the sister of my college boyfriend's roommate, George Hudnut. My old boyfriend, Scott Jeffries, shared a room with George in the Sigma Alpha Epsilon fraternity house.

His group of friends all had nicknames and for these two it was Nut-Job (due to George's last name having the unfortunate word *nut* in it) and Harpo (due to Scott's curly, blond hair). Most of the members of that fraternity were from small towns, but George hailed from Morton Grove, a suburb of Chicago. I was sure this was Judy.

I hadn't run into her in at least ten years. Did I want to get up and say hello? If George and Scott were still close friends, as I suspected, word of our meeting could get back to Scott. Did I want that to happen? I had to think about it. First of all, how did I look?

In my excitement to get my manuscript into the mail, I had neglected to put on any makeup. My mother had always warned me about running out without any blush on my cheeks. "After all, darling, you never know who you're going to run into," she had continued to warn me until I had finally secured a husband.

But there had been a few sunny days, after all it was late May, and I had acquired some color from the sun. I thought I looked fine, and I could mention having completed a book. But what about my marital status? Did I want that to get back to Scott?

I felt Scott would only wish me well. We had had a wonderful relationship and would have most likely have gotten married if it weren't for the small problem of our unborn children going to Hell. Sue had warned me. "You better find out where he stands on Jesus," she had remarked.

Then he told me. For the three years we were going together, he had secretly been attending church on campus every Sunday. That was no problem for me. He finally admitted that he wanted me to raise our children Catholic. That I wasn't willing to do.

I asked him flat out, "Do you think if the kids aren't baptized, and I don't accept Christ that we'll all go to Hell?" He admitted that in his brain he did not believe this, but that in his heart he had other beliefs. I could see the anguish in his face. We discussed getting married as Unitarians.

I knew my children would still be Jewish, but I could sense he felt his kids would end up in Hell. I could tell by the look in his eyes that he would be tortured. I couldn't do that to someone I loved. I suggested we see other people, hoping I would meet a nice, Jewish med-student.

Unfortunately for me, it was Scott who met someone right away. He met a nice Catholic girl who was from his small town in downstate Illinois. We both graduated and went our separate ways. He married a different woman years later. I would hear about him occasionally from George or Judy but hadn't run into either of them in a long time.

Here she was. She hadn't noticed me, and I doubted if she would have even recognized me. I never knew her very well. I could either leave or say hello. I got up to leave but then turned towards Judy. Her friends had already sat down, and she was putting Splenda in her drink at the counter.

"Are you by any chance Judy?" Too late to walk out.

"You look familiar," she said.

"Hi, it's Linda Grey." Her eyes widened, she smiled, and gave me a hug.

"Linda, how did you ever recognize me? It's been so long," she said.

I told her she hadn't aged at all, which she hadn't. She told me she'd read and enjoyed my columns. Finally, I got around to the subject of Scott, whom Judy still referred to as Harpo. George was still in touch with him. They saw each other at least once every year. Scott's kids were in college, he was still living in Belleville, and this was the shocker, his wife had left him for her old boyfriend, a retired pilot. Scott was divorced.

Should I mention I was separated? Would word of that reach Scott and result in a possible phone call? Should I pretend my marriage was just fine? I was flustered and didn't know what to say. If this were a page in my novel, I'd have time to figure out what to do, or I could write it one way, then go back and edit. This wasn't a novel. It was real life. Judy was telling me about her job and her kids, so I mentioned my three children and told her I had completed a novel.

When she asked me how I was able to do that with three kids, I casually mentioned that their father takes them on the weekends. I didn't want to explain, so I told her I had to run, and then I did, literally, out to my car.

Marv came by to pick up the kids. I told him I had sent out the entire manuscript, and that I was going to relax that evening. He told me he was proud of me and gave me a big hug, then left with the kids. He was once again sweet Marv.

What had I been thinking when I gave Judy the impression we were possibly divorced? I had complicated things enough by having Patrick to think about — did I really want to add an old love to the mix? I doubted that Scott would try to contact me anyway. I was remorseful that I had spoken to Judy. The best thing for everyone would be if Marv and I got back together, and things were pointing in that direction.

I was looking forward to reading one of my Barbara Pym books on the couch all evening. I was all ready to do that after having made myself a cup of Earl Grey tea and a plate of ginger snaps, however, I was interrupted by a knock on the door. It was Marv wearing an adorable smile and holding a bottle of champagne and a box of chocolate-covered strawberries. He had convinced Drake to take the girls bowling while he came over to help me celebrate and would pick them up later. It wasn't in Drake's nature to hang out with his little sisters willingly, but I knew he was rooting for his dad, and he would probably meet friends later anyway.

I poured the champagne into flutes and set them on the coffee table along with the ginger snaps and chocolate-covered strawberries. Marv sat down next to me.

"What's this?" he said as he pulled Drake's cell phone out from under a sofa cushion. "I'll give this to Drake when I pick him up," Marv told me. He held his champagne glass up to mine and proclaimed, "To my talented wife." We clinked glasses. "I have a surprise for you," he said and then went upstairs.

While I waited, I ate some strawberries. I checked Drake's caller ID on his incoming calls and found a frequent number of calls from a Marne Maples. I recognized that as a name of a family in the area. I thought Marne was their sixteen-year-old daughter. I made a mental note to ask Susan if her sixteen-year-old daughter, Kelly, knew the girl. Maybe Drake had a girlfriend he wasn't telling me about. I wasn't too concerned. I was feeling fine sipping my champagne, and my completed manuscript was in the mail.

Marv came downstairs, his footsteps heavy on the

staircase, and his face looked stern. His adorable smile had vanished. He was holding the wooden box I had given him when he first left. "I can't believe you could be so careless," he shouted at me. "You lost that ring with the stone my parents had brought from Europe. You just threw away my whole past. Nothing is sacred to you. This means nothing to you. You don't know what it's like. Your family was safe in America." I always hated when he got like this. His face was contorted and unappealing.

"What's wrong with you?" I shouted.

"You're what's wrong with me," Marv yelled.

"That's your surprise—turning on me?" I asked.

"I went into the attic because when you gave me this box of trinkets, I didn't take it to my apartment, I hid it in the attic. I had too many things to move out, and I just stored it up there. I figured the ring was safe in the box if you didn't have it, but it wasn't, because you were selfish and careless."

"You're acting crazy," I shouted.

"That stone was safely buried in the earth all those years. I give it to you and it's gone," Marv said with a snarl on his face.

"I feel terrible if it's lost. Why are you making it worse?" I guess Marv had no answer for that, because he stormed out. I was stunned. Things had been going so well. This was definitely not the new and improved Marv. This was the worst of the old Marv.

CHAPTER TWENTY-TWO

I *was shaking and had to calm down. I poured another glass of champagne. Feeling a little light-headed, I decided to call a taxi. I knew where I would wind up. In fifteen minutes I was standing at the entrance to Patrick's building. I told the doorman to ring Patrick. When the doorman asked, "Is he expecting you?" I told him I needed to interview Patrick right away, because he had just won the Jim Johnson Humanitarian Award, our paper was going to press early in the morning, and that I needed more details for my story. I insisted I was sure Mr. Rainey the Fourth would want to speak to me.*

"Mr. Rainey, Linda Grey is here to see you," I heard him say into the phone. "You can go up to the 12th floor. It's 12 East," he told me. I had never been to Patrick's place before. When I got to the 12th floor, Patrick was waiting at his door, David Niven-esque, in a green, silk, Chinese robe. He gave me a big hug and asked what was the matter. His place was tasteful, sleek, modern, and uncluttered. I sat down on a trim-lined, gray, ultra-suede sofa. Patrick handed me a whiskey. I was shaking, but I began telling him about my evening.

"And the thing is, he kept telling me not to worry about the ring. It's insured. The stone was hidden under his grandparents' house in Poland. His mother retrieved it after the war, and they brought it to America. All his history was in that stone. I feel terrible," I told Patrick.

Patrick put his arms around me. "It was an accident. Marv shouldn't add to your misery. If you were my wife, I would never want to see you unhappy. He still has his family history. It's passed down from generation to generation— *l'dor v dor*. And you've given him three great kids. He doesn't know how lucky he is."

I got up and started walking around. I was interested in seeing what his place was like. Everything was so neat. "I'll get dressed and we'll go out. It's a beautiful night," he said as he headed into his bedroom to change.

His teakwood bookcase was lined with hardcover books. Some were standing straight up with bookends and others were piled horizontally. There were some interesting plaster heads on the shelves along with several fleur-de-lis glass paperweights. The entire display looked as if it had been arranged by a magazine designer. As I ran my hand along a shelf (there was not a speck of dust), I noticed a hardcover copy of *The Loins of Moses*.

I recognized the cover art of Moses in a loincloth being pulled down by two women. I opened the book and found it was a first edition, and it was signed by the author, *Dearest Patrick, I couldn't have given birth to a better son. Love, R.R.* I hadn't seen a copy of the book since my U of I days. I opened the book to chapter six. I was curious if the text would have the same effect on me as it had when Marty Goldman read it to me in college. The story was still seductive and erotic.

A strange thought occurred to me. The descriptions of Moses seemed to fit Patrick. Could Katherine have had Patrick in mind when she authored the book? That was impossible. He would have been too young at the time that Katherine wrote this. As I read about Moses' adventures with the Medianite women, I could picture Patrick in his place. My head was swirling from the champagne and whiskey, from the emotions of my ordeal with Marv, and from Patrick's concern.

"Did I ever get teased by my college friends when they found out Katherine was Romana Roman? They used to call me *Romano* Roman. It was still supposed to be a secret in those days, but a friend read the inscription and figured it out," Patrick said as he entered the room wearing a tan, alpaca cardigan over a brown, button-down shirt and khaki chinos.

I could just imagine the teasing a younger and more innocent Patrick had suffered in his youth. He looked so sweet and adorable, I couldn't control the thoughts in my head.

"Let me read you my favorite chapter, chapter six," I said as I opened to page fifty-three. The narration was just as potent that evening in Patrick's condo as it had been years earlier. Before I knew it, Moses' desert robes were being peeled off as Patrick's alpaca cardigan and button-down shirt suffered the same fate. Just like the Medianite woman in the story, my neck was being covered with kisses. Touching Patrick's chest hairs, my fingers found their way to his gold Star of David. I remembered how intrigued I was the first time I saw that star.

Reading the passage had the same effect on Patrick as it had when Marty Goldman had read it to me in the deserted lounge at the Sigma Alpha Mu fraternity house those many years ago. Just like those days in college, reading this book led to groping, only this time it was tender, passionate, and held the promise of a future relationship.

After the way Marv had acted, I felt completely justified in allowing things to move forward. And move forward they did. Patrick's kisses were sweet and exciting. His touch was firm and tender. It had been a long time since I had been with Marv, and a very long time since I had been with anyone other than Marv. I had forgotten the thrill of the first time with someone new and wonderful, but soon, it all came back to me.

When we had finished recreating Moses' conquest of the Medianite princess or perhaps, more aptly put, the princess' conquest of Moses, Patrick suggested we get some sleep. I told him I couldn't stay over, much as I'd like to, because Marv stormed out without taking Drake's phone, and I thought Drake might stop by to get it. I didn't want him coming by late at night and finding me gone. What if he stayed waiting at the house, and I didn't come home?

I told Patrick I could take a cab home, but he insisted on getting dressed and driving me. His car was on the street, so we had to go out the front of the building past the doorman. I had neglected to tell Patrick that I had made up a story about him winning an award (which I had also made up and named after a popular radio newsman). I had made up the story because I knew I looked upset and didn't want to appear to the doorman or any passersby like some dramatic, helpless female. This way it looked as if I was desperate to get the final touches of my interview before my morning deadline. But I had forgotten about lying to the doorman and, before I knew it, there we were in the lobby.

"Congratulations Mr. Rainey," the doorman said, then turning to me he added, "I hope you got what you needed." I had.

On the ride home Patrick kept smiling at me. There was a twinkle in his eye. "Keep your eyes on the road," I told him.

"I can't help it. My eyes keep wandering over to your lovely face."

"I can't help thinking that Katherine based her descriptions of Moses on you. But that can't be," I said.

"Of course not. I was too little. She did base her character on my dad," he explained.

"But, wasn't that before they were married?" I was trying to figure out the timeline.

"Katherine has known my dad for years. There was nothing between them then, but she admired him. She always used real people as prototypes in her stories," Patrick explained. We pulled up to my house. Patrick put his arms around me. "If you need anything, let me know. I'll talk to you in the morning." He gave me a deep passionate kiss. "Everything's going to work out."

I entered my house and noticed that Drake's phone was still on the coffee table. So, he hadn't come home to discover me gone. That was good. I was emotionally and physically exhausted and went straight to bed.

When my head hit the pillow I started to go over the events of the evening. First I had felt satisfied that my book was on it's way to Barbara. Then I was delightfully surprised at Marv's thoughtfulness. Then I was surprised again. This time at Marv's 180 degree turn from sweet to bitter. My shock and sadness led me to Patrick's home. There, more surprises were in store for me. Patrick's tender and exciting passion, however, did not surprise me. While I was celebrating in my mind my new found lover, I was mourning the loss of my relationship with my husband of eighteen years.

I could feel my body relax in preparation for sleep. Just as I was about to fall asleep, my body twitched the way it sometimes does when I dream that I'm falling and am about to hit the ground. I opened my eyes, but instead of seeing my usual bedroom surroundings—armoire, desk, closet door—all I could see were sheepskin tent walls. I got up and walked out of the tent entrance. It was dark with only the light from some stars. I looked down and saw I was wearing a loose cotton gown that had no shape. There were other tents pitched nearby. The night was cool and the air was dry.

Patrick came out of a tent. He was dressed like Moses. "Linda, thank God I've found you. Come into my tent. We have to start right away. I am to have as many descendants as there are stars in the sky. But I can't do it alone. Hurry, into my tent," he said as he led me to the largest of the tents. Just then Marv appeared, also dressed in a loose robe.

"You can't go with him. You have your own family," said Marv. Patrick grabbed hold of one of my arms and started pulling me.

"She's coming with me," Patrick told Marv.

Marv grabbed my other arm and said, "Linda we

belong together. Besides, I have something to show you."
Marv reached under the opening in the front of his robe. I
could only imagine what he was about to show me when he
pulled out a purple, velveteen, Crown Royal bag. He opened
it. I looked in and what I saw made me gasp. Then I woke
up.

I sat at my kitchen table drinking my first cup of
strong, morning coffee laced with whole milk. I was trying
to remember my dream. The dream itself had left me with
a certain feeling of importance, but I could not conjure up
its contents. I tried a second cup of coffee but still nothing.
I decided to get my morning paper, but when I opened my
front door, it wasn't the Chicago Tribune sitting on my porch
steps, it was Marv.

He was holding a bouquet of roses in one hand and a
cup of something from Starbucks in the other. He looked up
at me. "Linda, I didn't want to wake you. I've been waiting
for you to get the paper. Can I come in? I know I was crazy
last night." I could see he was sincerely sorry, so I let him in.
Marv handed me the flowers and a grande cappuccino. We
sat down at the kitchen table, and Marv began apologizing
for his bad behavior.

I was conflicted. I was still angry at Marv, but I felt like
smiling over my secret—I had slept with Patrick. Of course,
I was also feeling guilty over the fact that this last argument
had sent me to Patrick's bed.

"Linda, I am so sorry. I wish I could take it back. I
was horrible. We've talked about this in group. Two steps
forward, one step back. I made all that improvement, and
then one little thing set me off, and I slid back. I don't even
care if the diamond is lost. I only care if I've lost you. And I
hope I haven't. Drake wanted to come by late last night to get
his phone, but I told him I'd get it in the morning. I had acted
so terribly, I was worried that I had pushed you into Patrick's
arms and maybe he would have been here last night. I didn't
want Drake walking in on anything, even though I consider it
would have been my fault if anything did happen. That was
the old behavior that I had learned at home. Still, I can't blame

my folks or the war any longer. I'm an adult and responsible for the way I act. I know I've come a long way, but then last night, I slipped up. I can't guarantee it will never happen again, but I'm trying with everything I've got to make sure it doesn't."

He still had that sorrowful look on his face. I didn't want to hold a grudge, wanted to move forward, but I had complicated matters by running to Patrick. I knew how much Marv had changed. Even with this episode of backsliding, he was still the new and improved Marv. He had worked through his anger and disappointment quickly and come right over to apologize.

In the past he would sulk, even if he was sorry, for days. Then I would hold a grudge for a few more days, so that every misunderstanding would last a week. This destructive pattern seemed to be a thing of the past. Maybe we could move forward. I was hoping a little thing like my sleeping with a new man wouldn't make a difference.

I agreed I would try to put last night behind me, and we shared my cappuccino. "Marv, if you thought there was a chance Patrick would be here why did you come in the morning?" I asked him.

"First of all, if he were here, I could handle it, but I don't think Drake could. I told you, I wouldn't have blamed you. It was my fault. Also, I knew if Patrick had come over last night, he'd know enough to leave very early. I wanted to straighten things out between us, so I waited till morning, but I didn't get any sleep last night," Marv told me.

"You better get some sleep. And don't forget Drake's phone. Did you know he has quite a few calls from some girl?" I asked Marv. He wasn't aware of it but didn't think it was a problem.

"I'm not saying it's a problem, but he'll be eighteen soon, and if he's sexually involved with an underage girl, he could be branded as a child molester just for having a girlfriend a year or two younger. I'm concerned," I told him.

"Drake's been opening up more lately," Marv said. "I think he's maturing. I'll have a talk with him. He's a responsible kid. Don't worry." Marv put me at ease when he said that. I had almost forgotten how he could take charge of things when I needed him to help me out. I gave him a hug goodbye, and he went home to get some very needed sleep. This time he took Drake's phone with him.

I was thinking what a difference a day makes. My completed manuscript was on it's way to a major agent, Drake may or may not have a girlfriend, Marv's family diamond was officially missing, and I had slept with the prototype for Moses' offspring. That's when I remembered my dream and got the urge to go to the bank.

I signed in with the same old man as usual. I sat in the private viewing room. Ever since I had kids, I've enjoyed my *alone-time,* even if it was just in the bank's private room. In fact, I especially enjoyed sitting there looking through my important things. And, because I do it so seldom, I'm always surprised at what I find. Since I've become a mother, I even like sitting in the dentist chair. I find it relaxing, being in a prone position, with no one fighting or yelling.

I was looking at the usual things: birth certificates, bonds, jewelry, etc., and there it was—the purple, velveteen, Crown Royal bag. Inside were the silver half dollar coins I'd had for years. I reached in and under the coins was a little ball of tin foil. I took out the foil ball, opened it, and saw what I was looking for—the diamond ring. The stone was loose. That was why I had wrapped up the ring before putting it in the bag for safe keeping. I had done that when I was pregnant with Delilah (which reminded me to bring home her birth certificate so she could prove to Agatha that she had been born).

Driving home, relieved that I had located the missing stone, it became quite clear to me—in the dream, Marv had been showing me the family *jewel,* not the family jewels.

I was torn. On the one hand, there was Marv—my husband of eighteen years, and the father of my three children. On the other hand, there was Patrick—young, sexy, handsome, and adoring. I needed to talk to someone, someone who knew a lot more about men than I did, so I made a phone call.

"Thanks for meeting me," I said as I buttered a small kaiser roll.

"Darling, it's always wonderful to see you, and I have some good news," Greg told me as he spread chopped liver on an onion roll. We were at Max and Benny's, a Jewish delicatessen on the North Shore. "But first tell me what's on your mind," he said.

"No, you first. I want to hear your news," I insisted.

"Oh dear," Greg exclaimed.

"What?" I asked.

"You're stalling. I can tell from the look on your face there have been developments. That particular look on the face of a married woman can only mean complications, therefore, I gather you and Patrick have tickled the ivories."

I was surprised by Greg's musical metaphor and insight. "How in the world could you tell that?" I asked.

"Darling, you know I know these things."

"I know," I agreed. "But how?"

"Just call it woman's intuition," he said.

"Very funny," I said, then I proceeded to tell him the events of the night before. Greg was particularly interested in the intimate details of the goings on in Patrick's apartment.

"Darling, tell me one more time — after you read the last page of chapter six in *The Loins of Moses*," Greg said.

"Honestly, you know that's not the point of all this," I said.

"I know darling, but my life is so dreadfully boring, romantically speaking. I do have news on the work-front, but I'll share that with you in a little while."

"So, what do I do now?" I asked.

"You've got this deliciously young, handsome dude, and you've got this darling, albeit not perfect, husband. Most people who don't know me might think I'd prefer wild sex with numerous anonymous partners, not that I don't enjoy the idea, but the truth is a long-term relationship with a soul mate—or in your case, *sole* mate, is really what I crave and, I think, what you crave also."

Greg was right. I just didn't know if Marv could keep on track, or if I could keep from holding grudges if he were to have lapses in his behavior. Katherine had been right. Patrick did adore me. He would never show me his ugly side. At least not until we were a completely devoted couple. Then, who knows? Isn't that how relationships work? You only hurt the one you love.

Was Marv my soul mate? Maybe he was the closest thing I had to one. Now I'd have to end things with Patrick if I was going to work this out. Patrick had told me he would call. Although my cell phone rang when I was at the bank, I was too preoccupied looking through my things to bother answering it. I knew it was Patrick, but for some reason, I was avoiding him.

"Thanks for your input. I know what I need to do, I think. But tell me your news," I said between sips of my chicken mish-mosh soup.

"I have a job I'm really excited about. And I get to sing."

"Fantastic. Is this something in musical theater?" I asked him.

"Sort of. It's in musical clean-up," Greg informed me.

I had no idea what musical clean-up was, so Greg explained that he would be doing what he had done along the highway, only this time he wasn't doing community service. He was being paid to lead volunteers at the Botanic Gardens. One of the docents for the Botanic Gardens had come across him leading the highway workers, and thought it would make the volunteers' work go by faster. The pay was decent, and he could set his own hours.

When I got home I started futzing around the kitchen: unloading the dishwasher, sweeping the floor, wiping the hand prints off of the walls—anything to avoid calling back Patrick. Then I remembered a call I had planned to make.

"What's the girl's name?" Sue inquired over the phone.

"It's Marne Maples. I thought Kelly might know her from school, or girl's sports, or something," I told Susan.

"That name does sound familiar. I'll ask Kelly. Are you okay?" Susan asked me.

"Sure, why?"

"You sound weird."

"No, I don't,"I said.

"Oh my God! You slept with Patrick," Sue said.

That was the problem with having good friends who go way back. You can't hide a thing. I had to fess up and tell her everything.

"Well, Linda, you've managed what every married woman dreams of — you got to sleep with someone new, but technically, it wasn't an affair because you were separated at the time, not to mention, your husband drove you to it, and now you can get back with your spouse, and even he would understand if you felt like coming clean. You are in the clear. You've eaten your cake, and you have it too." Susan certainly had an attorney's way of making it all sound legal.

"So you think I should get back together with Marv?" I asked her.

"I know Patrick is appealing: young and new, WASP and Jew. Sorry, didn't mean to rhyme. He might make a great husband. He also might secretly still want kids." I had thought of that many times, myself. She went on, "But you and Marv have always had a great rapport — between arguments. Now it looks like those arguments might become fewer and fewer. Do you want to give up a great husband just as he's improving? Because you know he'll be snapped up in a second."

"You're saying I should be grateful I was able to have a fling, and now I can have my marriage back," I said.

"Right. Wait a second, I think Kelly just came in." Sue left the phone for a few seconds. "I just asked her about Marne. She knows her."

"What did she say?" I was curious to find out.

"She said, 'Marne's a *nafke*.'" Susan said.

"Kelly said *nafke*?" I asked.

"Well, she didn't use that word. She said, 'Marne's such a slut.'" That wasn't reassuring. Marv would definitely have to have a talk with Drake. I wondered if Marv would be concerned, or, if like most men, he'd be thinking *that's my boy.* I knew I'd have to face Patrick. He had called my cell phone several times. I decided to take a warm bath and then face the situation.

I had started the water in the tub but forgot to take out Delilah's Barbie and Ken dolls. I made some tea, and when I came back to the tub the dolls floating around made my tub look like a miniature version of the Eastland Disaster. I didn't even bother to take them out. I just slipped in and added a few drops of lavender oil.

Relaxing in the tub, I went over recent events once again. Patrick had been so supportive, so adorable, I couldn't just drop him without explaining. I could see myself happy with Patrick, but I was troubled by my dream. Maybe he did want children. He had mentioned how lucky Marv is to have three great kids. I didn't think I had to make up my mind permanently, just yet. On the other hand, Marv was willing to work at making our marriage successful. The more I concentrated on my situation, the more confused I got. I got out of the tub ready to speak to Patrick.

Patrick had been worried all day up until I returned his call. I explained how Marv had apologized, and that I was considering working out my marriage. Patrick was understanding and supportive, but once again, convinced me not to jump to any permanent situation. He was willing to see me even if I was seeing Marv.

"You mean, may the better man win?" I asked him.

"He may not be the better man, but he'll be the luckier man," he answered.

CHAPTER TWENTY-THREE

The weather turned warm and humid. I was waiting to hear *from Barbara Crompton. Meanwhile, I started working on a second book, one with the same characters picking up where the first book ended. The Northside News had cut down on staff due to financal difficulties. So besides my regular column, I was editing other writers. Delilah started day camp, Agatha was taking a summer school class and still hoping to find a job, Drake was lifeguarding at The Barclay, a nearby condo building.*

I had been seeing both Patrick and Marv, nothing sexual with either of them, just lunch or an early dinner. I was in my office at the Northside News when I got a strange call. I could barely make out what the caller was saying.

"It's who?" I asked.

"Me, Millie," a whispering voice answered.

"Millie Meyers? I asked. She was the only Millie I knew.

"Yes, hi. How are you?" Millie continued to whisper.

"Millie, can you speak any louder? I can hardly hear you."

Millie explained she was at The Corner Bakery in Old Orchard. She had been enjoying a plate of ravioli and a coffee, when she overheard two men talking about a Linda. The voices sounded familiar. She took out her silver compact, the one with the silver test-tube on it, and looked in the mirror at the table behind her. The mirror reflected both Patrick and Marv sitting behind her.

"Listen for yourself," she whispered. She must have put the phone behind her. I could hear voices but couldn't make out what they were saying. "Did you hear that?" Millie asked me.

"I can't hear what's going on," I told her.

"Okay, wait ... They're talking about you ... Hold on ... Got it. Patrick said you deserve happiness and Marv told him you'd be happiest with your family back together. They're being very cordial. Wait a sec." Millie stopped talking, but I could hear restaurant background noises.

"What, what?" I was yelling to Millie, but she must have put down the phone.

"I'm back. Your husband's date from the wedding just showed up with another woman," Millie told me. I was thinking the other woman might be Katie's life partner. Millie continued, "Marv is introducing this other woman to Patrick. Her name is Nina." What the hell was going on? I decided to head out to Old Orchard.

"Can you wait there? I'm coming out to you," I told Millie.

"Sure. I have some work with me that I need to be reading, but I'll keep watching and listening."

"Great, you'll be my eyes and ears," I told her.

"As long as I'm no longer just a nose," she replied.

When I arrived at The Corner Bakery, I scanned the room for Patrick and Marv but couldn't find them. I saw Millie looking stunning in a green, silk jacket and tight-fitting jeans. She stood up and motioned me over.

"Sorry, you're too late," she said as she greeted me with a hug.

"Thanks anyway. There was nothing you could do."

"But I tried. I finally said hello to Patrick to stall them," Millie told me. When she realized they were all about to leave, she pretended to have just noticed them. Since she had sat at the wedding with Patrick and me, she approached Patrick first. She was hoping he'd remember her, but of course with her new face, he did not recognize her.

"At first, I told Patrick that I had sat with him at Lillian's wedding. He looked at me like I was crazy. I even told Marv and his friend Katie that I had also met them. They all looked at me like I was from another planet. I'm telling you Linda, this happens to me all the time. I don't know what got into me, but I finally yelled out *I had my nose fixed!* I think they were either all embarrassed that they didn't recognize me, or that I had yelled about my nose in public. They finally introduced me to Nina."

"Katie's girlfriend," I added.

"No, her niece. I tried to keep them all talking. I asked about Lillian and Barry, but of course, Marv's the only one who really knows Lillian and Barry. Marv told me he's Barry's cousin, and then I asked him to tell me how they met. They must all think I'm a lunatic. I just couldn't keep them any longer. But ..."

"But what?" I asked.

"But on their way out, I heard Katie ask Patrick if he could give Nina a ride somewhere," Millie said.

"So?" I was wondering what she was getting at.

"I don't know Linda, I just have a feeling they were trying to set up Patrick with Nina. I just have a nose for these things." Or she used to. I ordered a pumpkin muffin and coffee, and we talked some more.

Millie thought Patrick and I made a great couple, and that a new man would be more interesting than an old husband. She had a right to her opinion. She'd been there more than once. But she didn't have kids and that always changes the equation. I asked Millie to tell me about Katie's niece Nina.

"She's young, in her thirties, and very cute — a redhead," Millie told me.

I had to pick up Delilah from camp at Devonshire Park. I got there early, sat on a swing in the playground, and called Marv. I reached him on his cell phone.

"What were you doing out with Patrick?" I asked him.

"What did Patrick tell you?" He answered a question with another question, very Jewish.

"I haven't spoken to Patrick," I told him.

"How'd you find out? Did you see us?"

"Millie called me," I told him.

"That lady who said I met her at the wedding when she used to have a big nose. That Millie?"

"That's the one," I said.

"Boy, you really have a great network. Where are you? I can meet you."

I told him where I was, and that I would wait for him. I signed Delilah out of camp, and we waited in the playground. I was pushing her on a swing when Marv showed up.

"Daddy!" Delilah jumped off the swing and ran to him. He swooped her into his arms. "Mommy and Daddy. This rocks," she said. Marv's eyes met mine. I think we both felt guilty for putting the kids through all of this. Delilah ran over to some of her friends on the jungle-gym. I heard her tell them, "That's my Mommy *and* my Daddy."

"So what were you doing with Patrick?" I asked him.

"I asked him to meet me. I wanted to tell him that I'm serious about getting our marriage on track," Marv said.

"You didn't threaten him or anything?" I asked.

"Linda, are you nuts? I'd never do that, plus he's twice my size."

"What were Katie and her niece doing there?" I wanted to know.

"I won't lie to you or cover up. Katie and Nina ran into us. But the truth is, Katie knew I'd be there, and she had it in her head to introduce her niece to someone. Why waste a perfectly good man? I knew what she was up to, and I went along with it. Why not? He's a nice guy—just not for you," Marv said.

"And that's your decision to make?" I asked.

"No, just to hope for. Linda, I want us to get back together, and I'll do anything within reason to achieve that. Why shouldn't I?" He had a point.

We walked around following Delilah from one end of the playground to the other. She seemed even more animated and happy than usual. Marv explained he had had a long talk with Drake. Drake claimed he did not have a girlfriend— that he and Marne were just friends. They enjoyed the same kind of music. Marv thought there were quite a few girls with crushes on Drake. Drake denied it, but he listened when Marv gave him a lecture about abstinence and to at least be careful.

Then Marv told me something he had recently discovered. He had been relieved when I told him I had found his family diamond. He started talking to his folks about the stone, and discovered that after they came to America, they needed money to open their business, a discount soda pop store, so they sold the diamond.

Years later, they bought another diamond to replace the one they sold. They just gave this new diamond the same history. Then they bought yet another stone to give to Stuey if he ever got engaged. They were going to give him the same story (about it being under the house in Poland).

"So it was a real diamond but a fake," I said.

"I know. I said to my mom, 'so you just pretended it was the buried stone?' and she said, 'Why not? It's a real diamond, and a real diamond had been buried. It's the same only cleaner.'"

I finally heard from Barbara Crompton. She wanted to sign me. I was thrilled. Barbara loved my book and planned on submitting it to three major publishing houses, but first, she wanted me to do some rewrites.

"It's nothing major Linda. Just a few places need clarifying. I've written notes in the margins of your manuscript and FedExed the package. You'll get it tomorrow. I want the changes as soon as possible. Let's get going on this right away."

I was thrilled and nervous. Putting the finishing touches on my manuscript then having Barbara send it out felt like giving birth. It would be like cutting the umbilical cord. I was already beginning to feel post-writing depression.

Patrick wanted to celebrate and so did Marv, but I was on a tight schedule, so I agreed to lunch with Patrick the next day followed by dinner with Marv and the kids.

The next morning I got up early to read through my manuscript one more time. I would be getting Barbara's notes that day. I got Delilah up and took her to camp. By nine-thirty I was at my office. As soon as I stepped inside, Sara told me Katherine wanted to see me. I knocked on Katherine's door. She yelled for me to come in. I didn't see her right away. She wasn't at her desk or in her chair. Then I looked down and saw that she was trying to balance on a bosu ball. Lying on her back on the ball she kept trying to lift her legs off the floor, but she kept falling.

"Damn Pilates," she said. "It's supposed to straighten my inner core. Good Lord Linda, help me up." I offered her my hand.

"What's up?" I asked.

"Me," she answered as I helped pull her to her feet. "Also, I spoke to Barbara. She's thrilled to represent you. I suppose this means we'll be losing you at the Northside News."

"That's jumping way ahead of things. I haven't made a dime off the book yet," I told her.

"Good Lord, I'm relieved you're not making any plans to retire from here right now."

"Don't worry," I assured her.

"I would like to know what's happening between you, Marv, and Patrick. I hear Marv is playing matchmaker to my stepson."

"Obviously, I had nothing to do with it," I told Katherine.

"It is a new approach. You should feel very flattered that your husband will go to such creative lengths to get your boyfriend out of your life."

She went back over to the bosu ball and this time lay down on it on her stomach. Katherine began waving her arms and kicking her legs as if she were swimming. "What do you know about this young woman Nina?" she asked me while huffing and puffing.

"Just that her aunt is Marv's Children of Holocaust Survivors group leader," I answered.

"I'm sure Marv wouldn't introduce Patrick to anyone he didn't approve of. Marv has high standards," Katherine said. This was getting weird. I left her to her bosu-ball-swimming.

I worked at my desk until noon when Patrick arrived and took me over to a sushi restaurant on Peterson Avenue. We celebrated over spicy tuna and sake.

"You're going to have a great career as a novelist," Patrick said.

"Let me get one book published before I call it a career," I said.

"I have faith in you and so does Marv, who by the way, also happens to have a new career—making *shidduchs*," Patrick said as he was positioning his chopsticks between bites so they wouldn't dirty the tablecloth .

"So, what's she like, anyway," I asked.

"She's nice, smart, attractive, but she's not you." That was said in the nicest way I could imagine.

"But you plan to see her again, don't you?" I asked.

"I don't understand you, Linda. After what went on that night at my place, I thought we'd be moving things further along. Instead, you seem to be in cahoots with your husband about Nina." I noticed Patrick was repositioning his chopsticks and wiping the condensed water off of his water glass with a napkin before it dripped onto the tablecloth.

Maybe it was the sake, or the sashimi, or the chopstick-straightening, or the water-wiping, but before I knew it, I was trying to convince Patrick to give Nina a chance. I think deep down I had made up my mind to work things out with Marv, and I just wanted a happy ending for everyone, even Nina, whom I didn't even know. Patrick agreed to think about it. That made me feel better about getting together with Marv and the kids for dinner that night.

Chapter Twenty-four

Agatha and Delilah were setting the dining room table, while Drake was straightening out the living room. I had collected all the bills and stray papers and put them away in boxes, hoping I'd remember to take them out and pay them later, but I knew there was a good chance they'd be forgotten, and then I'd be assessed with late fees. That was the chance I always took when I tried to straighten the house.

"The fork goes on the other side, Loser-rina," Agatha said to Delilah.

"Mommy, she's changing everything I do," Delilah complained about her sister.

"Just put a fork and knife on a napkin and place that in the center of each plate, okay?" I said to both of them.

"Fine," said Agatha sneering at her little sister.

"Fine," said Delilah giving her sister an equally dirty look.

"Girls, girls," said Drake putting an arm around each sister, "you don't want to make Dad realize he'd rather be home alone in his apartment. Do you?" The girls nodded. "All right then, let's everyone act like we always get along."

"Fine, I'm a good actress," said Agatha.

"Fine, me too," Delilah agreed.

There was a knock on the door. Drake answered it. I was in the kitchen filling a crystal pitcher with ice water. Drake came into the kitchen and handed me a package. It was my manuscript with notes from Barbara.

"Good," I said. "I can't wait to see this." I started ripping open the envelope. Drake grabbed it from me.

"Mom, I know you're excited about your book, but could you please give it a rest, just for tonight? This is really important to me. I want us all to have a nice family dinner," Drake said. I promised Drake I wouldn't think about my book until after his dad left and put the manuscript in my top dresser drawer.

We all worked hard to get the house in having-company-over order. Marv arrived carrying bags of Thai food. The girls ran up to him and hugged him.

"You brought so much food," I commented as he put the bags down on the dining room table.

"It's a good thing. Looks like you're having company or did you clean up for me?" Marv asked.

"For you. Tonight you're company," said Delilah.

"I'd rather just be one of the family," Marv said.

"Don't worry Dad, you are just one of the family. Mom doesn't usually make company bring their own dinner," said Drake.

The rest of the evening went on in the same manner — easy-going, funny patter. When Marv went to the refrigerator to get a bottle of club soda, he took something else out instead. He held it in his hand and asked me, "How long have you had this? How long have you had this?" I looked at what was in his hand. It was a twice-baked potato left over from another meal. He was asking twice because it was twice-baked. When I realized this I laughed. We were back to our old selves. He knew I would get the joke.

I had forgotten how Marv and I could be in perfect sync

with each other when we wanted. He could easily finish my sentences, our sense of humor and references to things being so similar. The kids fit in all this beautifully. They alternated between making witty remarks and then spewing familiar insults at each other. I could sense everyone was enjoying themselves.

There wasn't much left of our meal. Wooden sticks that had recently held chicken satay were in heaps on the dining room table. Styrofoam boxes that had housed mango salad, pad Thai, pad-si-yew, and tofu green curry were piled up on the kitchen counter.

"I have an idea," said Marv. "It isn't summer if we don't get dessert at Dairy Star." The kids agreed that summer meant ice cream at Dairy Star. Since I didn't want to be responsible for ending summer early or causing an untimely snow drift, I agreed we should all go. After the kids fought over who should sit where in the van and I strained my voice yelling at them to buckle their seat belts, we headed over to the small, open-for-summer-only outdoor-stand.

Dairy Star, which opens at the beginning of summer, had been around for years. It was frequented by all sorts of folks: families, teens, motorcycle gangs, etc. It had originally served not just ice cream but also burgers. One year the grill broke down, and the owners found if they got rid of the grill, they could make it into a kosher ice cream stand. So they did.

Word of it going kosher spread through the neighborhood like cream cheese on a toasted bagel, and when Dairy Star opened up that next summer, they were packed. I remember when this first happened, groups of ultra-orthodox men in black hats showed up for heaps of swirled soft serve.

The customers who had been going there for years had no way of knowing it was now approved by the Chicago Rabbinical Council. I think they suspected groups had been bussed in from Amish country. Everyone was staring at each other, but as the weeks went by things normalized, and before you knew it, the bearded rabbi was handing napkins over to the Hell's Angels member who was dripping cherry syrup on his black leather chaps.

I parked the van on a side street, and we walked over to Dairy Star. Marv got in line while the kids, and I looked at the pictures of different ice cream creations. The line was its usual eclectic mixture: some Muslim women wearing head scarves, Orthodox women in light brown, page-boy shaytels, a blonde woman with a bad perm and a rose tattooed on her shoulder, some black-hatters, rowdy teens — the whole lot.

The outdoor tables were filled so Marv, the kids, and I sat on a bench against the small building's brick wall and ate our ice cream. We had to be attentive to our desserts because the heat was quickly melting our confections. It was the usual contest of a Chicago summer versus our tongues. The summer heat was winning. I went to the counter to grab badly needed paper napkins.

As I grabbed a handful someone said, "Linda, hi." I turned and saw it was Chaya Malka, the woman who had returned the gift cards and other things from my stolen purse. She was waiting in line with her husband and a group of children of varying age.

"I never thanked you for that lovely basket from A Schtickle Nachas," she said.

"Chaya Malka, you didn't need to thank me. I was thanking you. How are you and your family?" I inquired.

"Wonderful, Baruch Hashem," she answered. "My husband just got a job. We're celebrating," she added.

We're celebrating too, I thought, but just said, "Mazel Tov!" I returned to my family to distribute the napkins but was a little late in Delilah's case. She had dripped chocolate ice cream down her beige shirt. I started blotting it with a napkin.

"It's okay, Mom. You can use spot remover, and if it doesn't come out, well, it'll be like a tie-dye shirt," Delilah said reminding me of her positive attitude that I so admire.

"Delilah, you look great in chocolate," said Chana Leah approaching us.

"Thanks. It's my favorite color," Delilah said. Her face was covered with chocolate.

"It suits you," Chana Leah said then looked at me. "Linda, how are things?"

"Fine. Baruch Hashem." *When in Rome,* I figured. "How was your trip?" I asked her.

"To Jamaica? It was wonderful," she said. In a hushed tone she added, "No one there that we knew."

"You must have had a great time," I whispered back.

"I sat around the pool all day in a one-piece bathing suit drinking margaritas," she whispered back at me then joined her family in the line.

Agatha and Drake were talking to some teens they knew, and I heard Marv say goodbye to a man wearing a knit kippah. I signaled to everyone that we needed to get home. It was getting late.

"Who was that man you were talking to?" I asked Marv when we got in the van.

"Dr. Melman. He does nursing home care. He told me that Yossel Lapudus' father passed away. Tomorrow's the last night of shiva," Marv said.

I usually read the obituaries, looking first at those marked with a Star of David, but lately I'd been writing so much, I had let the newspapers pile up without catching up on the news of the newly demised. Marv worked at one of the nursing homes owned by Yossel Lapidus. I knew how Marv hated to attend funerals and shivas without me. I agreed to go with him the next night.

Marv tucked Delilah in bed then came into the living room to say goodnight to the rest of us. He gave me a hug and kiss, said, "I'll see you tomorrow," then he left.

Agatha said to Drake, "They have a date tomorrow."

I said, "We're going to make a shiva call. That's hardly a date."

"They're going together. That's a date," Agatha said to Drake.

"Yeah, that's a date—a cheap date—but a date," Drake agreed.

Marv showed up at eight o'clock. It was a humid evening and my hair was kinking up. "I like your hair like that. It shows off your pretty face," Marv said. "I hope they've finished the prayers. I always feel like I don't know what they're doing."

"Shouldn't they be finished by now?" I asked.

"Who knows?" Marv said.

We walked the four blocks over to the Lapidus home. I told Marv about the notes Barbara had sent me. Her notes were minor, mostly problems with continuity that could be easily corrected. Still, at 300 pages, I needed the time to sit down and do the work. Marv told me how proud he was of me.

There was a crowd of women and a few men standing outside the Lapidus home. I could see in the window that the men were still praying in the living room. We waited outside in the heat. When the prayers ended, some people who had been inside the house left, while those waiting outside, entered the brick Georgian-style home.

Marv and I went into the house. The mirrors were covered with sheets. Yossel and his brothers were in the living room sitting on cushions on the floor or low seated chairs, as is the custom for Orthodox mourners. There were rows of folding chairs set up to face the mourners. Marv and I sat down on the chairs and listened as Yossel told his visitors about his father's sudden demise at the age of ninety-four. Yossel recounted his failed attempt to rouse his father from a nap, the calling of the ambulance, the transportation on the stretcher, the sitting at his father's bedside, and his father's peaceful passing from this world to the next.

During pauses in Yossel's story, people would get up to leave. They would stand, say some prayer in Hebrew, and back out towards the front door. At the door, there was a small table with several bowls that had the names of different charities written on them. As the visitors approached the door, they would place a few dollar bills in one or several of the bowls, then leave.

I was concerned that we didn't know the prayer to say,

so that we could comfortably leave. We had only been to one other Orthodox shiva house, and that one had been so crowded that we had stood in the back and left surreptitiously. Orthodox shiva houses are much different than other Jewish shiva houses which are more like social events with a lot of schmoozing and eating.

I whispered to Marv, "Do you know that prayer?"

"Something about being comforted amongst the mourners of Zion." I knew that much.

Now new people were arriving and sat next to us. Yossel got up from his seat and went into the kitchen while one of his brothers started telling the new visitors about his father's death. "Yossel couldn't wake Dad from his nap," one of the brothers began.

"Isn't this where we came in?" Marv whispered to me. I wanted to leave and hoped perhaps a large group of people would be leaving, and we could just stand with them, as if we were part of the group, while they blessed the mourners. But only one or two people at a time seemed to be exiting. It would be difficult to sneak out with two strangers. A man and woman stood up, looked at Yossel's brothers, and started saying the mourners' blessing to them. The brothers thanked them, and the couple left.

"Maybe we can just say ... *whatever they said, goes for us too*," I whispered to Marv.

"I wonder what they'll serve us for breakfast in the morning," Marv whispered.

A group of men came in the front door as Yossel was coming out of the kitchen. The men stopped him and were conveying their condolences.

"We're gonna make a break for it," Marv said. "Follow me." We got up and went over to Yossel before he had a chance to return to his seat. We told him how sorry we were for his loss. Yossel thanked us. We turned to leave. Stopping at the bowls for *tzedakah*, Marv told me he had locked his wallet in the car. I checked my wallet but didn't have any cash, so I dropped a Blockbuster gift card in the bowl for a Yeshiva in Jerusalem.

CHAPTER TWENTY-FIVE

he weather was hot and steamy, but I refused to complain, because, like a true Chicagoan, I knew come January I'd be longing for the heat. Besides, things were good at home. The kids were getting along unusually well, Marv and I were acting like we did when we first met, and I was enjoying revising my manuscript.

I was also looking forward to my trip to Lake Geneva with the girls. This is when we always catch up on each other's lives and even brainstorm family problems. Since we all met in college, it's almost like time-travel back to the past. We let down our guard, and are once again, our old selves before we had careers, husbands, or kids.

"What do you think of Barbara's suggestions, and how was the shiva house last week?" Katherine asked me from behind her desk as her head lay on a stack of folders, while a nine inch candle burned in her left ear.

"First, could you explain why you're doing this?" I asked her.

"This?" Katherine pointed with her left hand to the candle. "Good Lord Linda, I'm ear-candling."

"I know what it is. I've written about alternative health. Why are you candling?" I asked her.

"To clean out my ears and improve my sinuses."

"I have no idea about your sinuses, but your ears seem to be in perfect order. You seem to hear about everything," I told her. "Do you know the Lapidus family?"

"No, but I have a girlfriend who was crashing the shiva house, Lucille Greenbaum, she really needs to meet someone. She recognized you. She also informed me that some rabbinical students in Israel will now be able to rent the latest *Star Wars* movie."

"I'd hoped no one saw that," I commented.

"But things with Marv are good?" Katherine inquired. "Lucille thought she saw the two of you holding hands and giggling on your way out." There seemed to be a lot of smoke coming from Katherine's ear candle.

"We both enjoy a good shiva house," I told her.

"Patrick is stopping by. He wants to talk to you," Katherine said as a huge billow of smoke encircled her head.

"Katherine? Linda?" It was Patrick. He had just walked into her office holding a briefcase in one hand and a water bottle in the other. "What the hell is going on?"

"Owww," Katherine yelled. Her hair had caught fire. Patrick quickly emptied his water bottle on her head. Katherine jumped up from the desk. Her hair was soaking wet, but the fire was out. I watched the candle roll off the desk onto the floor.

"Are you all right?" I asked her as she scurried into her private bathroom. Patrick looked at me and rolled his eyes.

"Patrick, don't you dare roll your eyes," Katherine yelled from the bathroom. Patrick looked adorable and confounded.

"Katherine's been ear-candling," I explained

"So I see. She really needs a hobby," he commented.

"I heard that," Katherine yelled from the bathroom.

"You could give knitting a shot, or crocheting. How

about cross-stitch?" he shouted towards the bathroom.

Katherine came out of the bathroom with a robe over her clothes and a big, fluffy, white towel wrapped around her head. She walked towards her desk. When she spotted the candle on the floor, she bent down, one hand on the towel around her head to keep it from falling off, and picked up the candle. Katherine looked at it then tossed it in the waste basket under her desk. It made a loud *thunk* as it hit the bottom of the basket.

"I think my sinuses are better after all," she said.

Patrick and I walked over to a little coffee shop around the corner.

"I'm worried about Katherine. Dad's been traveling around the Middle East buying and selling maps. They need to spend some time together," Patrick told me.

"She should take a week off and meet your dad in Palm Springs," I suggested.

"He'll be back there in two weeks, but with the reduced staff at the newspaper, Katherine doesn't think she can get away," Patrick said.

"She's been asking me to take on more responsibility. Maybe when I come back from my girls-getaway I can help out," I suggested.

"You're the only one she trusts to fill in for her. And your rewrites will be finished by then, won't they?" he asked. I told him I was sure they would be completed soon. I wanted to help out Katherine, if that meant pitching in more hours at the paper, I was willing to do that.

"How are things with Marv?" he asked.

"He's been sweet. We're getting along well, and the kids are happy," I told him.

"Nina tells me Katie thinks the world of Marv," Patrick said.

"And what do you think of Nina?" I asked him.

"She's really nice, interesting, attractive, but I still miss you." Patrick told me that he and Nina had been out together about three times, but that he was taking it slow. I noticed he was refolding his paper napkin so that the edges were aligned perfectly.

Maybe I was being overprotective of Patrick, but if he and I were ending things, I wanted to make sure he would be moving in the right direction. I couldn't see the sense of Marv setting Patrick up with a woman if there wasn't the possibility of a future in it. Even though Marv's matchmaking had been done without my knowledge, I had now become a co-conspirator in the pairing of Patrick. I wanted to make sure that Nina was worthy of my ex-lover's attentions.

"Do you think Nina is interested in having children?" I asked him. Patrick explained Nina had confessed that her last relationship ended because her boyfriend not only had two teenage children, but he had something every divorced mother is looking for in a new man—a vasectomy. Unfortunately that's not what a never-married, childless woman in her early thirties is looking for. Her boyfriend did not want any more children, and Nina knew she wanted at least one child. She decided to move on.

"I guess I would like a family," Patrick admitted. "I know how important I am to my dad and Katherine. Wouldn't she just flip for a grandchild?" Patrick asked me. I had to laugh thinking of Katherine in that role. She would be adoring and meddling and probably at her best. Patrick continued, "I would just love to have a kid who called Katherine *Bubbe*."

"You should have a child if for no other reason," I said.

"Linda, I don't know if anything is going to happen with Nina, so don't be so sure that you're rid of me just yet." I started to say something, but he just went on, "I understand that you want to work things out with Marv. And I know he's a great guy, but I also know you won't stand for any backsliding on his part. There still is a chance that you and Marv will not stay together."

"A slim chance," I said.

"That's all I'm saying. Basically, I do believe couples should work things out if they can, especially if there are children involved. Just look at Katherine and my dad. They've always worked out their problems," Patrick said.

"Of course, they don't live in the same state."

"And, they're rarely in the same hemisphere—still, they adore each other," he noted. I promised Patrick I would offer to help out if Katherine wanted to go to Palm Springs in a few weeks. I would be back from my trip by then, my book rewrites would be finished, and Marv and I would, hopefully, be settled back into a state of married bliss, or the realistic equivalent of such a state.

The next few days went by smoothly. The kids were happy, Marv was happy, I was happy, Patrick was happy, Nina was happy, and Katherine didn't set her head on fire. It was a good week.

CHAPTER TWENTY-SIX

HOW do you like that? So I offered to sleep on the pullout couch because, as you know, she always has to have her own room." I was on the phone with Jen who was explaining to me that, at the last minute, Lillian had decided to join us.

"I thought you said Lillian would never leave Barry so soon to come with us," I said to Jen.

"That's what I thought, but in fact, she is leaving him, has left him."

"You mean she's leaving Barry to come with us?" I wanted clarification.

"She's left him."

"She's left him?"

"She's left him!"

"So soon?" I was stunned.

"I'm telling you, I was shocked. She called me two days ago and asked if there was an extra room. I told her we have adjoining suites, and I would check. She wants to join us. So, of course, I was surprised. Then she went into this long list of injuries Barry has acquired since their marriage. Did you know they came back from their Costa Rican honeymoon with Barry's arm in a sling and his face covered with hives?"

"So he's accident prone. Why are they splitting up?" I asked.

"You know how Lillian loves everything to be so perfect. She's sure that Barry is subconsciously having accidents to sabotage the marriage. All these accidents throw her schedule off. She takes his injuries as a personal affront."

"I hope she knows what she's doing. She's hardly given this marriage a chance," I said.

"I know. Anyway, she's joining us for the first time in years. But there are no more rooms available."

"You don't have to take the pullout couch. I'll take it," I offered.

"Why should you take it?"

"I shouldn't. Lillian should take it, but we all know she won't come if she has to sleep on a couch. You've done all the work making the arrangements. I don't mind. Besides, I've had my own bed for the past year. You never get a bed to yourself," I said.

Word of Lillian's breakup spread faster than women's hips after childbirth, because the second I hung up with Jen, I got a call from Doree. "Can you believe it?" Doree asked me. "She told Jen getting married was a big mistake." *So was sending a gift before the first anniversary.*

Doree went on, "It'll be great having all of us together on the trip."

"It'll be a riot," I said.

"And, I have a surprise," Doree said.

"You're engaged?" I asked.

"No, but I'm still seeing Habib. He's darling. Something else."

"Then, you've gone blonde," I said.

"Who told you?"

"I just guessed. Everyone seems to be doing it." My call-waiting started clicking. "Hold on," I told Doree. It was Mitzi on the line. "That's Mitzi, I'll talk to you later."

"Say hi but don't tell her about my hair. I want to surprise her in Lake Geneva." I got off the line with Doree and continued with Mitzi.

"Doree says hi," I told Mitzi.

"Can you believe it?" she asked.

"Unbelievable," I said.

"I'm sure she'll tell us more on the trip. I can't wait to see everyone. And, I have a surprise," Mitzi said.

"You went blonde too?" I asked.

"No. What do you mean, too?"

"A lot of women seem to go blonde at this age. It's an epidemic," I said. I didn't want to give away Doree's surprise.

"I'm not telling but you'll see. Don't forget to bring some pictures from college. Jen always brings her albums, and we should bring some old photos," Mitzi suggested.

"I think I do have some stuff in the attic, but it's such a mess up there." I promised Mitzi I would search through my attic.

Later, I received an e-mail from Caro. She was stunned at the news of Lillian's breakup, she could not wait to see us, and she also had a surprise which I figured to be some new cosmetic procedure. I would have to remind myself to be on the lookout for fuller lips, tighter neck, or higher breasts.

"You will definitely have the extra column before you leave on your trip?" Katherine asked me.

"I promise I'll be finished with the story about *Wabe Sabe*," I assured Katherine as we walked out of the Northside News building together. We were both heading to our cars, which were parked on Lincoln Avenue.

"Good Lord, what the hell is Wabe Sabe?"

"Wabe Sabe is the Japanese notion of honoring the flawed and impermanence in things by preferring the imperfect to the perfect," I explained.

"Like not repairing the Liberty Bell?" Katherine asked.

"That would be one example," I agreed.

"Or not getting Botox injections?"

"Another good example," I assured her.

"I'd never get those shots in my face anyway. My husband would hate it. You know how Paddy loves old maps," Katherine said.

"You're no old map," I told her. She still had naturally flawless skin, and you could tell she had been a great beauty in her youth.

"You know what Paddy tells me? He says, 'Katherine you are one handsome woman.' Good Lord Linda, no woman wants to be called handsome. It makes her think she looks like Howard Keel. Anyway, I like this Wabe Sabe philosophy. I hope it replaces Feng Shui," Katherine said as she stopped in front of her black metallic Mercedes SLK 350 Roadster with gray leather interior.

"It's certainly different than Feng Shui," I said.

"I need to get rid of all my Feng Shui books. They're cluttering up my entryway," she said as she got into her car and took a black-and-gray paisley scarf out of her glove compartment. The scarf matched the exterior and interior of her SLK Roadster.

Katherine turned on the engine and pressed a button, which automatically lowered the car's top into the trunk, turning the hardtop into a convertible. While this was happening, she put the matching scarf on her head, tying it under her chin. Adding dark glasses, she reminded me of Jacqueline Kennedy Onassis. Katherine waved to me and yelled, "Via con Dios, baby," as she gunned the engine and sped away.

I was heading over to Wholly Frijole, a small Mexican restaurant on Touhy Avenue, to meet Marv for an early dinner. Delilah had a play-date after camp, and Agatha and Drake had plans with their friends. This was just going to be the two of us.

"Hola," the hostess greeted me. I told her there would be two for dinner, and she seated me at a table as a waiter brought over chips and salsa. I took out a small notebook from my purse and started jotting down ideas for the Wabe

Sabe article while I waited.

"Writing about me, I hope." That was Marv's voice. I looked up and he was standing at my table, his wet hair dripping down his neck. He gave me a kiss.

"It's not that hot out," I said referring to his dripping wet head.

"I just took a shower at the JCC," he told me.

"I didn't know you still workout there?" I said.

"I don't. I've been trying all day to take a shower. They're having plumbing problems in my building. The water was off today. The building manager told me it could take two weeks to replace all the pipes."

"Two weeks! But the kids will be staying with you in a few days," I said.

"The manager, Hernando, assured me there would be water from six till eight most mornings."

"The kids will never be up that early and Agatha needs at least forty-five minutes in the shower to cream rinse all her hair. She'll be miserable," I said.

"She'll be fine," Marv told me.

"But I won't. I can't enjoy my girls-getaway if my kids are constantly calling me to complain. What's the point of getting away?" I asked.

"I'll make it clear no one's to call you," Marv said.

"Why don't you just move into the house while I'm away?" I suggested. I could see Marv's face light up.

"That's a great idea," Marv said.

"Of course, Katherine always tells me I'm a genius."

"You are a genius, but I have to admit, I was thinking of the same solution. I just didn't want to be presumptuous," Marv admitted. "Maybe I could stay after you return," he added.

"It might turn out that way," I said as I closed my notebook and put it back into my purse.

"What were you working on when I interrupted you?" Marv asked.

"An article on Wabe Sabe." I could see the puzzled look on Marv's face. I continued, "It's like when you have a treasured wooden table and it gets a crack in it—instead of replacing it—you just keep displaying it." I could tell he was getting it. "Basically, it's the Japanese art of not fixing things," I said.

"It's the art of not fixing things but the Japanese didn't invent it?" Marv said.

"Then who did?" I asked.

"Jewish husbands," Marv said. I laughed. Marv took my hand. "Linda, I really think it's time we got back together. It can't be easy juggling all the kid's schedules alone."

"You're always helping out," I said.

"It's not the same as being there in the house. If you need to work late, I'll already be home," he said. The waiter came over and took our orders: red snapper and garlic mashed potatoes for Marv, chile rellenos with rice and beans for me.

"You want to move back home because it'll be convenient for me?" I asked.

"It will be more convenient for you but that's not why. I want to move back into the house because we belong together. It's *beshert*. I know it, you know it, the waiter knows it." As Marv said this, he nodded toward the waiter who was at another table. The waiter must have seen this from the corner of his eye because he came back over to our table and approached Marv.

"Would you like something?" The waiter asked in his Mexican-accented English.

"Permanence," Marv answered.

"I'll have to ask the chef," was the waiter's reply.

CHAPTER TWENTY-SEVEN

I *had no problem finishing all the neccesary changes in my* *book. The hardest part was coming up with a title. Because* *my characters Fran and Glenn are torn between their parents'* *past in Europe and their feelings about being first generation* *Americans, I decided on* Red, White and Bluestein *for the book's* *title. I had e-mailed the changes and title to Barbara.*

"Linda, I just love the title. It's perfect. I really connect with the characters' struggle between their Jewish and American identities. Oh, and I love all the *Yiddishkeit,*" Barbara told me.

"I'm so glad. I wasn't really sure if you'd get all the Yiddish references," I admitted into the phone.

"But Crompton was originally Kaufman until my grandfather landed at Ellis Island," Barbara said. "Didn't Katherine tell you?"

"She never mentioned it," I told her.

"Of course not. She's a *shiksa.* Only Jews tell you who's Jewish, you know, *the list* ... Tony Curtis, Kirk Douglas ..."

"Dinah Shore," I added.

"Christopher Columbus, allegedly. I don't think Katherine has *the list* memorized," she said. I assured Barbara that I would mentally add her to *the list* in my head. Barbara explained that my novel was now ready to be sent around. She believed she could garner interest from several large publishing houses.

I was thrilled by Barbara's news and wanted to call Marv, Patrick, Katherine, Jen, and the rest of the girls, but I had the house to myself and so preempted the urge to make phone calls with the urge to take a relaxing bath.

This bath would be perfect. I placed a cup of Constant Comment tea with a shot of Amaretto in it on the tiled tub deck. Next to that, I placed the book I was currently reading, an English cozy novel from the '70s, and a pair of reading glasses. The top of the water was filled with soft bubbles and the entire bathroom smelled of lavender bath gel. Slowly, I lowered myself into the tub. The water was warm and inviting.

I was enjoying my cozy novel as well as my tea. I decided to shave my legs, but of course, I had forgotten to place a razor by the tub. I could see a pink disposable razor at the sink. I had to get up out of my bath to get the razor. I was careful not to knock over my teacup. However, on my way back into the tub, I knocked my book with the heel of my right foot. The book fell into the water. I grabbed it quickly and threw it onto the counter. It wasn't soaked too terribly, but I could tell when dried, the novel would be a lot thicker than the author had intended.

I didn't get to read my book, but I finished my tea, shaved my legs, and exfoliated with a lavender sugar body scrub. Getting out of the tub, I was careful not to kick my teacup off of the tub deck. I patted my body dry with a fluffy, white towel then applied lavender body lotion to my legs. Sitting on the tub deck, I rubbed my calves together. I always love the way they feel when they are newly shaved and moisturized. My legs felt like silk. I thought a bikini wax was in order and hoped I could get an appointment before I needed to leave on my trip.

I called Marv to tell him the news from Barbara. "I know you're going to get a book deal soon," he said.

"How do you know that? You haven't even read it," I said.

"Not because I haven't wanted to," Marv reminded me.

"I'll leave a copy for you in the house. You can read it while I'm away," I told him. Marv was looking forward to being in the house with the kids. I was curious; how would he react to the parts in the book that dealt with the children of Holocaust survivors?

After speaking to Marv, I called Patrick. He seemed a little down. "What's wrong?" I asked him.

"I guess I'm a little jealous of Marv moving back into your house," he said.

"First of all, he's not moving *back* into the house—he's moving into the house just until I get *back* from my trip," I said.

"And second of all?" Patrick asked.

"What do you mean?"

"You said, 'first of all'. You can't have a first-of-all without a second-of-all. It's like an outline—you can't have A without B," Patrick told me.

"You're right. My second-of-all was that it's not my house, it's our house," I explained.

"So, you're prepared to have Marv back in the house— the two of you back together?" Patrick asked. I admitted that I didn't know the answer to that question just yet, but I would be figuring it out during my time away on my trip. I asked Patrick how things were going with Nina. He was still seeing her, but he didn't sound very excited about it. I didn't know if he was curtailing his excitement for my benefit, or if he really was so unenthusiastic about Nina. Patrick was, however, very excited about my news from Barbara.

"It's great to see someone doing what they love," he said. I *was* doing what I love. I was taking care of my kids and writing. Those are things I love. But, did I love being married to Marv? That was a question I was hoping to answer. I knew I really enjoyed being with the new and improved Marv, and that I could never go back to the old Marv. But I was also aware that Marv did not want to go back to the old Marv — the Marv that got angry over every little thing: the open jelly jar, crumbs in the diaper bag, my choice of cultery, my parking skills, the way I grated parmesian cheese, my hairstyle (even though it's my hair!). That was the old Marv, the critical Marv, the negative Marv, the Marv who behaved like his father. The new Marv had learned to be himself by getting rid of his baggage. I was proud of him. I had the urge to share this with my friends and wanted to call them, but I was going to see them soon.

First, I had to find those pictures from college I promised to bring, so I went up into the land of no return — my attic. To get there I had to go upstairs and walk through Agatha's room, which was like a war zone — land mines of accessories scattered everywhere.

I was barefoot and my feet hurt from stepping on eyeliner pencils, earring posts, and the plastic tops to lipstick cases. I decided to put on a pair of Agatha's shoes but couldn't actually find two shoes that matched, so I slipped my right foot into a sequined covered mule and my left foot into a denim covered clog. Walking in two different shoes caused me to limp a little, but at least my feet were protected. I walked through the door in the back of Agatha's room that led into the attic.

Switching on the light, I proceeded into the cavernous abyss. When I venture into the attic, I am always surprised by the fact that it is even more cluttered in person than it is in my imagination. Over the years Marv, the kids, and I had all piled things into the attic that we did not have the guts to part with. And it now looked like we were a pretty gutless crew. There's a small ski slope near my house called Mount Trashmore because it was originally a garbage dump that was later covered with grass. My attic looked like Mount Trashmore before it was covered over.

I carefully made my way over to the far end of the attic

where I had originally put things when I first moved in with Marv. I sat down on a big pile of shoes, stuffed animals, and old towels and began sorting through a box of stuff from my single days. I finally found an old photo album that had AEPhi written on it in black magic marker. I opened the album. The pictures that were once glued began to fall off of the pages.

There I was with my long Heb-fro with Jen and Mitzi posing on either side of me. We looked young and cute but not really much different than today I thought. I found a picture from a U of I Mom's Day weekend of Caro, Jen, and me with our mothers, and I noticed that we all grew up to look just like our moms did back then. There were other photos from our sorority dances. We all looked so happy. Why not? Our skin was glowing and our flesh was firm.

I got up to go back downstairs to pack the album. I looked down and spotted a lime green box. I remembered that box. I knew what was inside, so I sat back down and opened it. There they were — all the letters. I opened one up. The crease made it hard to read, but the handwriting was large, and if I held the letters at arms length, I could still decipher them.

The page was filled with words of love and adoration. *I* was the missing piece to his heart. *I* was the music in his life. *I* was the laughter in his gut. I was referred to as *My most adorable darling*. These were the letters I received the summer Caro, Mitzi, and I traveled around Europe together. It was the summer we were going into our senior year of college. We figured it might be our last summer to play and not have to work, knowing once we graduated, we would be thrown into real life and the work force.

Jen and Doree had traveled the summer before, and so Jen had mapped out a route for us. She told us we could give the addresses of the American Express offices in Europe to our families and friends so that letters would be waiting for us at the offices in each city we visited. Telephoning from Europe in those days was an expensive and almost impossible proposition. The three of us had looked forward to getting mail as soon as we got into each new town.

There were the occasional letters from parents, siblings, and friends catching us up on the latest gossip at home. But it was the letters with the return address from Belleville, Illinois that I had looked forward to receiving that summer. At every American Express office, I would get at least one, and more often two or three, letters from Scott Jeffries . All of Scott's letters were filled with declarations of love and how much he missed his most adorable darling.

I wondered what Scott looked like now. Would he still be darling with his tight swimmer's body and curly gold hair? Most likely, he would have put on some middle-aged excess weight and would have closely cropped gray hair. Maybe he was bald or had a bad comb-over. I wondered if he heard from George that I ran into Judy.

I hadn't seen Scott since we broke up. I was twenty-one at the time. We had almost gotten together years later. It was when Drake and Agatha were in preschool. I had received a call from Scott. He needed to come into Chicago to take a deposition or something related to one of his legal cases. He thought it might be nice if we had breakfast together. I agreed. Marv was fine with this and even picked out what he thought I should wear—a very expensive blazer and sexy-fitting jeans. Marv wanted me to look my best.

Then I got another call from Scott. He had mentioned to his wife that we were getting together for breakfast, and apparently, she went ballistic. So, he had promised her he wouldn't see me, and he cancelled. I had thought his wife sounded nuts and insecure. What did she think was going to happen over breakfast? Did she really think Scott would be caressing me over a plate of ham and eggs, or that I would be fondling her husband beneath the table under my serving of lox, eggs, and onions?

As I sat there in the attic perusing Scott's passionate letters, I thought how sad it is that young people today will never receive love letters. No one even writes in long hand anymore or sends real letters on stationary through the US Postal Service. All correspondence is done by instant-messaging or e-mail with letters instead of words. What would a love letter in e-mail look like? *I luv u* signing off with a *LOL* (laugh out loud) and then a :) (sideways smiley face).

I was glad I had a cache of love letters. I even had some from other young men, plus many from Marv during our courtship and the early days of marriage. But those were in another part of the attic, and I would have to search for them later. I stuffed Scott's letters in the album then shoved the aging photos back into the album as well and headed downstairs to pack them with the rest of the things for my trip.

I put the album in my Samsonite rolling suitcase. I took my blue tankini out of my drawer and packed it. Seeing my tankini reminded me that I had to get a bikini wax. I was leaving for Lake Geneva on Friday. It was already Wednesday. I called Hair Here, the salon next to Starbucks in the mall where Mrs. Morrie lived. I hadn't been there in a long time. Lina, the receptionist, answered. I told her I needed an appointment for a bikini wax as soon as possible. There was nothing for today or Thursday, but there had been several cancellations for Friday morning.

"Who is this?" Lina asked.

"It's Linda Grey."

"Oh, hi Linda. I have you down for a bikini wax at ten on Friday morning."

As Lina was talking to me, I was looking at my hair in the mirror. I needed to do something different with it. I was willing to try something new.

"I need a new style—something different," I added.

"We can handle that," said Lina.

I got a call from Jen. She wanted to know if I would mind driving to Lake Geneva alone. She wanted to leave very early Friday with Doree, so they could get a round of golf in at the resort. Doree and Jen are the only ones of the group who golf. I didn't mind at all. I looked forward to the relaxing drive with my sunroof open and an old Ella Fitzgerald CD playing.

Thursday morning I went to the Jewel Food Store to pick up some treats for the trip. Jen had given each of us an assignment of what to bring. She tried to assign each of us our favorite foods. Jen was bringing Kellogg's Sugar Frosted Flakes, red licorice, and M&Ms. Doree was in charge of wine and cheese. Mitzi was bringing diet Coke, diet ginger-ale, and diet Seven-Up. Lillian was bringing a bottle of champagne. Caro was in charge of bringing face-masks, nail polish and polish remover, and I was to bring coffee, Half & Half, and any hard liquor I might desire.

I also bought plenty of fruits, vegetables, and healthy prepared foods for the house. I didn't think Marv would be doing any cooking with the kids. He would most likely be taking them out for meals, but I wanted them to have good choices of things to munch on when at home.

I put the groceries away and froze the Half & Half. Since I was now running late getting to the Northside News, I decided to check my office phone for any messages. There were the usual messages from some local PR people asking me to write about their client's restaurant, store, production, or strange invention. But there was another voice, a voice from the past.

I recognized the raspy voice and southern Illinois drawl immediately. The voice said it was Scott, then added Jeffries, in case I didn't know which Scott, then added from Belleville, in case I didn't know which Scott Jeffries, then finally adding "From your past," in case I didn't know which Scott Jeffries from Belleville was calling.

Scott said George told him that Judy had run into me. He also said he was going on a golf trip with George and Daryl. Scott thought I might remember Daryl from his fraternity house as someone who used to be known as Dangles for reasons he didn't want to get into.

"Anyway," Scott's voice said, "after our golf trip, I'll be visiting George and his family in Chicago for a few days. I'll be there August second. I hope we can get together. I still owe you a breakfast." He left his cell phone number.

I hadn't heard that voice in so long; I could hear my heart thumping. I didn't know if it was because I still had feelings for Scott. I knew Judy would most likely get word to

Scott that she had seen me but hearing his voice after reading over his letters just caught me off guard.

I didn't know if I should see Scott after my trip, or if I should even return his call. I still had to get into the office to do a little work before my trip. Everything would get worked out during my girls-getaway. I could still share everything with my friends. That knowledge helped calm my beating heart, and soon I was in my office attending to newspaper business.

"Good Lord Linda, Barbara tells me she's ready to send your manuscript around town," Katherine said to me in her office over the buzzing of some electronic sounds.

"What's that noise?" I asked.

"Come look," she said. I walked around her desk to see that she had her feet in some vibrating device.

"It's massage and reflexology. I'll leave it here for you when you come back. You can use my office. You are coming back, aren't you?" Katherine looked concerned.

"Of course. I don't even have a book deal yet."

"Because Paddy is expecting me next week," she said.

"I'll be here. I promise."

CHAPTER TWENTY-EIGHT

Every summer I start imagining myself relaxing at the pool days before I actually leave for my trip. The closer the trip gets, the more I imagine. This was the evening before my trip, and I could almost taste the chlorine. I knew during the trip that my friends and I would do what we always do — talk about how relaxed we are and about how this will last us for the next three or four months, but the truth is, as soon as we get back, and the kids start fighting, all the good the trip did us is shot, and we need another vacation, which we won't have again for another year, unless we take a family vacation, and believe me, that is no vacation.

So our summer getaway will have to do, even if we only pretend it will do. I couldn't wait, although it was quiet in the house because Drake was working, and Agatha had taken Delilah to the park.

There was a knock on the door. It was Marv.

"Excited for your trip?" he asked as he kissed my nose and brought a box into the house.

"What's this?" I asked

"Goody bags for you and the girls." I looked in the box. There were six floral-printed gift bags. Each one was filled with foot care items: heel-softening ointments, scented foot powder, pumice stone, nail clippers, wooden foot-massager, and chocolates in the shape of feet.

"They'll love it." I gave him a kiss on his nose. I made us some tea and went over our plans for Friday. I would drop Drake off at his lifeguarding job, take Delilah to camp, then get my bikini wax and hair done at Hair Here before leaving for Wisconsin. Agatha would probably sleep all day, Drake could walk home after work, and Marv would pick up Delilah after camp.

"And you and the girls will be painting your toe nails and eating chocolate feet by 2:00 PM," Marv said accurately detailing my immediate future.

Friday morning I gave Agatha a kiss goodbye. She was sleeping so soundly she didn't even notice. Then I dropped off Drake at The Barclay. He gave me a kiss.

"Have a great trip mom and don't bother to call me," he said.

"Save a lot of lives today," I said.

"Right. It's just a bunch of old ladies who don't want to get their hair wet. They just sit at the edge of the pool and dangle their toes in the water. I'll be bored as usual," he said as he got out of the van. I watched him walk through the building doors. He was tanned, tall, and broad-shouldered. It was a good thing it was just a pool full of old ladies, or everyone would be in love with him, pretending to drown in the shallow water.

"I'm going to miss you so much, but Daddy and I are going to have so much fun. When you come back we can all play together," Delilah said as she gave me a big hug around the neck. I signed the sign-in sheet, and she joined the other campers.

I had been in such a rush that I hadn't packed my car and figured I'd do that after dropping off Delilah. Then I planned to head straight out to Lake Geneva after my bikini wax and new hairdo.

After I put my suitcase and the goody bags in my van, I went back in the house for the Half & Half that I had frozen the night before. I put that in a small cooler I had filled with ice. I put the cooler in the van. I also packed the gourmet Jamaican coffee I had bought and a bottle of fifteen-year-old Dalwhinnie Scotch whiskey I had purchased plus a couple of cans of real Coca-Cola. I thought I must be the only Jewish woman in the world who didn't drink diet colas.

Marv pulled up just as I was about to leave. "I thought you would have left by now," he said. I told him I was on my way to the salon. He explained that he was bringing his suitcases before going to see patients. He opened his trunk which was filled with suitcases and boxes.

"What's all this?" I asked.

"My things."

"But so much."

"If I'm moving back I might as well bring what I need," he said.

"What do you mean moving back?"

"We decided it was a good time for me to move back," he said.

"No. That was a *maybe* it was a good time to move back, not definitely. Let's see how the five days go," I said.

"But that's with the kids not with us. How do we know how it will go with us if we're not living together. That's what we discussed at dinner," he said. He looked as if he was getting frustrated.

"I didn't agree to that," I said. Now he looked angry. The corners of his mouth were curving downward. He was getting that look that I hated, the old Marv look.

"You are pissing me off. What the hell do you think you're doing? You agreed and now you're backing out. I've had it." He started putting his bags back into his car.

"What are you doing?" I asked

"I'll be back with Delilah later and I'll only stay until you come home. Then you'll be free of me." He got in his car, slammed the door, and then drove off.

I drove over to the strip mall on Touhy. Before heading

into Hair Here, I took a swig of Dalwhinnie in my car. After all, I wouldn't be on the road until after my bikini wax and haircut. Then I called my office phone and picked up Scott's phone number from his message, which I had saved in my voice mail. I was nervous and took another sip of Dalwhinnie. Scott didn't answer, so I left a message telling him I'd be out of town for a few days but would love to see him in Chicago and to call me after the first of the month.

Now I really needed a bikini wax and good hairdo. I tried not to look upset as I entered Hair Here. I noticed Mrs. Morrie under a hairdryer reading *In Style*. Lina greeted me.

"Have some champagne. It's our ten year anniversary at this location," she said. What the hell? I took the glass. I was feeling pretty light-headed. Lina called over someone named Trina.

"Linda, this is Trina. She's new here and a real artist." Lina handed Trina my ticket. It had some writing on it that I couldn't make out.

I followed Trina into the private room. Trina handed me a paper apron, and left. I could smell the wax burning. I took another sip of my champagne and relaxed a little. I lay down on her lounge chair. There was a knock on the door. It was Trina.

"Linda, are you ready for me?" she asked.

"Wax away." I was feeling no pain but not for long.

I could feel Trina applying the wax with a flat wooden stick. The wax was warm but didn't burn. She did seem, however, to be spending way too much time on that area for just a bikini wax, but maybe I had had too much to drink to judge time. I decided to just relax and enjoy the few moments I had lying down like I do at the dentist's office.

Then Trina started the pulling. It was weird. She was pulling in zigzaggy directions. It was all happening so fast. She pulled with her right hand, she pulled with her left hand. Then her right again. Then her left. I screamed.

I heard Lina on the other side of the door. She was telling someone they couldn't come in. I heard Marv say, "But, I'm her husband." The door burst open. I jumped up. Marv was standing. His mouth was agape. I looked down. My pubic hairs were in the shape of a bolt of lightning. I screamed, "A lightning bolt?"

"Actually, I call it the *Hairy Potter,*" Trina said.

"Don't you love it?" asked Lina.

"Are you crazy?" I said to Trina. Trina handed me the job ticket. It said on it *bikini wax — wants something different.*

"Isn't it different enough?" Lina asked.

"Are you sure you can drive, because I can take you and pick you up Wednesday. It's no problem," Marv said as we sat on the cozy chairs in Starbucks.

I assured him I was fine. After all, I had just downed two cups of coffee.

"And your," Marv lowered his voice, "lightning bolt isn't still stinging?" he asked.

"I'm fine," I assured him. "Your calendula ointment is fantastic."

"And you do forgive me?" he asked.

"I do," I said, and I did forgive him.

After our fight, Marv had realized that he had overreacted. He desperately wanted to apologize to me. He knew I'd be at Hair Here. When he arrived, I was already in the room with Trina. At first, he sat and waited, but he barged in when he heard me screaming. After my initial shock at the realization that I was sporting a lightning bolt, Lina and I reconstructed what had happened.

When I called for my appointment, I had asked for a bikini wax which usually means *a little off the sides,* but while I was on the phone looking unfavorably at my hair, I told Lina that I wanted a new style, something different. She had no way of knowing that I meant a new style for the hair on my head. That's why Trina gave me my new look, which had put me in such terrible pain. Fortunately, Marv, always at the ready, had calendula ointment in his doctor's bag in his car. The ointment seemed to put the fire out. He apologized profusely for his bad behavior. Lina and Trina felt terrible about the mix-up but couldn't seem to control their laughter.

Eventually, I had to laugh and so did Marv. I had still wanted a new hairdo so Lina called Gino, the owner, who was taking a coffee break next door at Starbucks, and told him to drop everything and give me a cut, which he did. He gave me a fabulous cut, and my curls fell flatteringly around my face. There was also no charge. Marv waited, and then we went next door for coffee.

There we sat holding hands. "You did get a great new look—two great new looks," Marv said. We both laughed.

"Wait till the girls see it," I said.

"You're going to have a great time," Marv said. "I'll have my things out when you return," he assured me.

"Maybe you should stay," I said.

"I'd love to more than anything, but I want you to be sure. I'll move back slowly, when you're ready. I'm the one who moved out. Moving back will be on your terms," he said. He was sweet and so new and improved. We hugged goodbye, and I was off to meet my friends in Lake Geneva.

I opened the sunroof of my van. Ella Fitzgerald was singing *That Certain Feeling*. Who would believe that at my age I would have three great guys interested in me? It felt good, and I didn't have to decide anything just at that moment.

Driving to meet my friends, I suddenly felt a relief that, no matter what decisions I would make, I would always have their unconditional support. Would I cut the ties with Patrick, refuse to see Scott, and make reconciliation with Marv final and complete? If Marv was backsliding, becoming the old Marv that I could no longer tolerate, I might want to see if there was still any chemistry with Scott, or I might wind up seeing Patrick.

Whatever decision I would make, here I was driving with the sunroof open, on my way to the safety-net of my old friends. I had a great new haircut, and I was sporting a lightning bolt on my crotch. I couldn't help thinking life is full of possibilities.

For information about this book's Reader's Guide, as well as a
peek at Caryn's next novel, please go to www.westridgepress.com

Photo © Karen Hirsch

Caryn Bark is a writer, comedienne, humorist, essayist, and playwright. She is the creator/performer of the critically acclaimed one woman show *Diary of a Skokie Girl*, which has played to sold-out audiences in Chicago, Kansas City, Little Rock, Phoenix, and Canada's Winnepeg Jewish Theater. She has appeared on Lifetime Channel's *Girls' Nite Out*, has opened for Joel Grey, and worked for HBO and Comedy Central. She has been heard on NPR's *The Savvy Traveler*, has been a frequent guest commentator on Chicago public radio station WBEZ, and a regular on Marie Osmond's radio show, *Marie and Friends*. She has performed at comedy clubs across the country, including Catch a Rising Star and The Improv. Her TV credits include The Gong Show, where she was quickly gonged by JP Morgan, which, thankfully, ended Caryn's brief singing career. Caryn's articles have been published in numerous magazines and newspapers. She is featured in the anthology *The Unsavvy Traveler: Women's Comic Tales of Catastrophe*. Ms. Bark studied at Chicago's famed Second City. She currently performs her evening of comedy *What's So Funny About Being Jewish* at JCC's, synagogues, and fundraising organizations across North America. Caryn lives in Chicago with her husband Fred and their three adorable (what else?) children, Chapman, Dashiell, and Tallulah. This is Caryn Bark's debut novel.

For bookings contact Smoked Fish Productions
smokedfishprod@aol.com
773-764-8936